Chi' Raq Gangstas

Romell Tukes

Lock Down Publications and Ca$h
Presents
Chi'Raq Gangstas
A Novel by *Romell Tukes*

Romell Tukes

Lock Down Publications
P.O. Box 944
Stockbridge, Ga 30281
www.lockdownpublications.com

Copyright 2020 Romell Tukes
Chi'Raq Gangstas

First Edition January 2021
Printed in the United States of America

This is a work of fiction. Names, characters, places, and incidents either are products of the author's imagination or are used fictitiously. Any similarity to actual events or locales or persons, living or dead, is entirely coincidental.

Lock Down Publications
Like our page on Facebook: Lock Down Publications @
www.facebook.com/lockdownpublications.ldp
Cover design and layout by: **Dynasty Cover Me**
Book interior design by: **Shawn Walker**
Edited by: **Lashonda Johnson**

4

Stay Connected with Us!

Text **LOCKDOWN** to 22828 to stay up-to-date with new releases, sneak peaks, contests and more…
Thank you!

Submission Guideline.

Submit the first three chapters of your completed manuscript to ldpsubmissions@gmail.com, subject line: Your book's title. The manuscript must be in a .doc file and sent as an attachment. Document should be in Times New Roman, double spaced and in size 12 font. Also, provide your synopsis and full contact information. If sending multiple submissions, they must each be in a separate email.

Have a story but no way to send it electronically? You can still submit to LDP/Ca$h Presents. Send in the first three chapters, written or typed, of your completed manuscript to:

LDP: Submissions Dept
P.O. Box 944
Stockbridge, Ga 30281

DO NOT send original manuscript. Must be a duplicate.

Provide your synopsis and a cover letter containing your full contact information.

Thanks for considering LDP and Ca$h Presents.

Acknowledgments

First and foremost, all praises are due to Allah. Shout out to my pops and family for all the good vibes and support. Shout out to everybody from Yonkers, NY, D-Block, Ruff Ryders, Smoke a.k.a Moreno I love you, bro. Shout out to Killa from Peekskill and the fam out there. Shout out to my guy Spice from Newburg. You always keep it 100, bro, respect. Shout out to O.G. chuck from Brooklyn and Tom Dog. Shout out to Muscle, Going Fitness we like this fitness shit. Shout out to B.G, Beast, Rugar, Snap, and all my Patterson guys. Big shout out to Lock Down Publications, the game is ours. Y'all saw my vision and helped me. Sky's the limits! Much love to all. To all the readers fucking with me, I'm always pouring my heart out and give you the hottest hood shit out there. I can stand on that word! Black Lives Matters we are all Kings and Queens.

Romell Tukes

Prologue

Chicago Juvenile: Four Years Prior

"Pass me the ball!" Boss yelled to Malik who was at the top of the indoor basketball court in their unit.

The young man was playing three on three as they did every weekend in jail as other inmates placed side bets with their commissary food and stamps.

Malik was dribbling the basketball in front of another inmate playing hard defense on him. Malik was a good shooter, but his ball handle was trash.

"Yo', Malik!" Animal yelled posted up by the rim waiting on the rebound with other big men.

Like taking candy from a baby. As soon as the ball left his hand, Boss came out of nowhere and blocked his shot, slapping the ball back to Malik.

Malik saw Boss wide open at the three-point line again, everybody was on the sideline yelling for him to shoot but this was the last shot and there was a lot of money on the game.

He passed the ball to Boss and two niggas rushed him trying to make him nervous as he shot the ball in the air.

Everybody was quiet until the ball swished into the net making a wet sound, everybody went crazy. Even a couple of guards standing outside the fiberglass window were placing bets with the other C.O.s because Boss was the best player in the building.

Later That Night

"Damn I can't believe we won five-hundred dollars in these goofy nigga's commissary," Animal said as him, Malik, and Boss all sat at a table eating a big meal they'd cooked together to celebrate their win.

All three men had been in the Juvenile Center for close to a year. They became the best of friends even though they were from all different sections of the city and different gangs.

Boss was seventeen years old, he was an All-American high school basketball player who caught a robbery outside of a Western Union. Malik was sixteen years old, a high school drop-out since the 9th grade, he robbed a low-level drug dealer who ended up snitching on him. Animal was a seventeen-year-old giant in for a gun charge, robbery, and two shootings that were acquitted because the two victims refused to come to the felony hearings.

"I was looking like M.J, on the Bulls in ninety-one," Boss said, making a shooting pose.

"Nigga, fuck out of here. Joc, you were looking like Dennis Rodman in ninety-five," Malik said in his Chi-Town slang.

"I hope that was before he got on that freaky shit, Joe." Boss started laughing.

Chi-Town niggas used the term Joe and Moe to address other just as New York niggas say so and B, and D.C. niggas say slim and down south niggas say bruh and shawty.

"I've been thinking bro when we get out, we need to form a crew and get to a bag because niggas is dying broke. I lost six of my guys in ten months," Animal stated.

"Six niggas, I lost eight," Malik added

"I lost eleven, bro," Boss stated shaking his head thinking about his young niggas he'd lost to dangerous Chi-town streets recently.

"We are from different hoods, so if we do this, we gotta stand on this shit," Boss said seriously because the city was full of gang wars.

"Till death do us part," Malik and Animal said at the same time.

"What's our name and what are we going to do?" Boss asked.

"I don't know, Joe, but we have to be smart," Malik said knowing the feds had the city on lock.

"How about we rob and kidnap the city King Pens and gangstas, we got money," Boss whispered, and they all looked at each other.

"Like on some random shit?" Malik added, liking the idea.

"What if that shit backfires, we're as good as dead," Animal said as everybody started to rethink the idea.

"If that comes to it then we drill shit bro that ain't nothing new. We all been dripping shit," Boss said, making sense.

"I'm down," Animal said.

"I'm down too, Joe," Malik stated.

"Okay, so we are all in bro," Boss said smiling.

"What's going to be our crew name?" Malik said.

"How about Chi'Raq Goons?" Animal said.

"Nah, how about Assassins?" Malik said, thinking of an assassin movie he saw last week.

"Nigga, this ain't the *Accountant* movie but how about Chi'Raq Gangstas?" Boss said everybody looked at each other.

"Yeahhhh," Animal said.

"That's it then we established but when we all touch, we gotta give it some time to get our feet wet, Moe," Boss stated.

"I agree," Malik stated.

Animal nodded while they switched conversations as other inmates came over to their table talking about the basketball game earlier.

Romell Tukes

Chapter 1

Southside, Chi' Raq: Present

Boss eased the tip of his dick into her girlfriend's extra tight walls and wet pussy trying to loosen her walls to accommodate his ten-inch monster.

"Uhmmmm shhh—" Rosie moaned slowly inching her thick thighs open as he went deeper into her wetness.

Rosie looked into his eyes, as he started pounding her pussy out the frame hitting her G-Spot, they both struggled to control their nut.

"Uggghhhhh—ooohhhh fuck, baby!" she screamed as she watched him place her legs over his shoulder and give her long hard deep strokes.

"Take it, baby." Boss sucked her titties as they bounced back and forth.

She was trying to fuck his dick as she was about to come. "I'm cummminggg, papi!" she yelled, biting her bottom lip, grabbing the pillow, and squeezing it as she climaxed.

Rosie creamed his dick with her cum, when he pulled out, she slid down on her knees and wrapped her thick, juicy lips around his thickness, sucking real sloppy.

She bobbed her head up and down while using her hand to twist his dick as she continued to deep throat him and he revealed himself. Rosie swallowed all his kids like a true trooper, she smiled at him as he laid down so she could do her thing.

Sha sat on his dick wiggling her round ass trying to slowly take it inch by inch.

"Uhhhhh ohhhh, yesss—" she moaned as he grabbed her ass cheeks, spreading them apart.Her pussy lips wrapped tightly around his dick as she bounced up and down making her titties jumped with every motion.

"Fuck—" Boss said as she rolled her hips in dance mv popping her pussy on his dick as her tight grip almost made him lose control. "I'm about to nut, baby, slow down," he said as she picked up the pace and his hips thrust into her. She bounced faster and faster until they both climaxed at the same time.

"Oh, my God. I have to get ready for work. I'm hopping in the shower real quick," Rosie said in her Spanish accent as she put on a robe and kissed his soft lips before walking to their room to the shower in the hallway.

Boss loved morning sex it was so passionate and intense whenever it was with his wifey who he'd been with for close to eight years now ever since they were little kids.

Tyrell Jonson a.k.a Boss was born and raised on the southside of Chicago in a section known for killing and violence. Boss was raised in a single mother home with a little brother who shared the same mother but a different father. Boss pops Ty Stone has been in federal since he was two years old on the Rico murder charges, and drug trafficking king pen status 848.

Without a father to look up to, Boss looked for guidance in the streets and that's what he found as he became a Gangsta Disciple member, who had a large number of members. Boss was twenty-one-years old, tall at 6'1 height, lean built, with long dreads and tattoos over his chest, neck, and arms. He has brown-skin, hazel-light eyes, and a handsome face with a nice smile.

In high school, Boss was an All-American basketball player by the time he was in the 11th grade he'd already received a full scholarship to D-1 division schools.

Unfortunately, he caught a case and was sent to juvenile, losing his basketball dreams, and ended up resigning his GED in jail. He lived with his girlfriend in an apartment in the hood blocks away from where he grew up. Boss didn't have a job, he sold pounds of weed to local hustlers and smokers thanks to his plug.

Boss needed a blessing because he was down a bag with bills, car notes, food, and basic living he was tapped out, and Rosie only made but so much money at her job as a home aid nurse. Boss, Animal, and Malik remained tight throughout the years since they started Chi'Raq Gangsters. They were never able to put their plan into motion because life took unwanted turns once, they were released.

Boss's mom kicked him out of her house, so he went to live with Sofia who had her own place, but she needed help so Boss hollered at his big homie and started to mount exotic weed.

Malik ended up getting a job at a coal plant, just to stay out of the way. Animal caught a new bid for a gun and another shooting which landed him with three and a half years in Stateville Prison. Animal came home a couple of weekends ago and Boss had yet to reach out to him since he was out.

Boss went to take a quick shower with his girlfriend before he started his day, his phone started ringing off the hook with customers requesting some new kush with purple strings.

Romell Tukes

Chapter 2

Lamaran Street, Southside

Animal was in the park on the monkey bars on the hottest day of the summer in his hood Lamaran Street better known to most as C-Block and Black Disciple. Animal was shirtless, showing his six-pack abs, muscular chest, and big arms doing pull-ups, clips, and push ups to maintain his well-defined body. Since being home from prison things had been hard, and he came home to nothing. He was still wearing his jail sneakers and underclothes. The only people who looked out for him were Boss and Malik since day one. He hadn't got a chance to holler at either one of them yet, but he planned to tonight.

Animal's real name is DeWayne Gary, twenty-one years old, very big at 6'4 and two-hundred and seventy pounds all muscle from lifting weights and being heavily into fitness. He was black as midnight, with low cut waves, dark beady eyes, a small cut under his left eye, tattooed teardrops under his right eye, and handsome with big hands.

He grew up with an older sister and a mom who used to smoke crack when he was a baby, but now she was just a coke head. His father ran off on them when he was young, so his mother did her best trying to raise two kids on welfare and section 8 and EBT food stamps cards.

Animal's neighborhood was known for violence, O' Block was one of the city's worst neighborhoods in Southside, Chicago. It was the home of the BDs for years which was one reason why Animal joined the gang. Every day in prison Animal talked about his crew Chi'Raq Gangstas and how their name would soon take over the Southside

While most of his homies laughed at him, he used to laugh back hoping one day they would be some of his victims since the inmates loved bragging about how they were all selling keys and counting millions of dollars.

Animal was now thinking was he just leaving in a dream while in prison-like most niggas and wishing on a fallen star. Aimal had come up with a plan to get some money before he reached out to his best friends Boss and Malika. Animal hit the track and started running laps flying past women who were eyeing his sexy body with lust wishing their husbands were hot like him.

Chicago Heights

Rosie was driving in her brand-new, clean, white Acura Sedan with tinted windows, on the way to work in Chicago Heights, a section outside of the main city in the outskirts. She hated her job as a Home Health Aid, but she'd been doing it since she graduated high school. At twenty-two and with no plans to go to college she wanted to live an independent life and that's what she was doing. Rosie was 100% Puerto Rican, her family were all raised in Chicago and most of them were all Latin Kings and Queens and Latin Disciples or Manic Disciples, Spanish gangs in the city that were dangerous and seriously known for getting money and brutal murders.

Her brother King Mike was the head leader of the Latin Kings in Chicago, her father in prison was a Latin King, her mother was a Latin Queen as well as. Rosie wasn't a gangbanger, it was just in her blood and who she was. Growing up on the Westside of Chi'raq in a hood called K-Town was rough because they were the only Kings in a Vice Lord hood, but they learned to respect them and eventually started to get money together.

Rosie's brother King Mike was a big-time drug supplier in the city and on the outskirts in places like Harvey Riverdale, and Robins, I.L. Boss was the love of her life, she worshipped the ground he walked on. They have been together so long they became each other's better half over time, and they shared a strong connection. She caught him cheating a couple of times but after a couple of fights, they got through it and just learned to work on their love life, and their happiness.

Rosie was a dime and every man's dream. Wherever she went dudes would holler at her, but she would turn them down before they could even finish their sentence because she already knew what all men wanted. Her greyish-green eyes were what caught niggas attention, then her high yellow skin, nice titties, big phat ass with her small waist made her curves look like a coke bottle figure on steroids. She had nice thin eyebrows, high cheekbones, nipple, and tongue piercings, and long silky bleached her with brown streaks.

It was 3 p.m. when she pulled into Ms. Daisy's driveway in a nice quiet neighborhood, she was thirty minutes late, but Ms. Daisy didn't even remember what day it was at times when she was off her meds.

Rosie entered the house to start work which took a lot of patience because she had to clean the house, bathe the patient, change diapers, cook, give them meds and look after them until one of their family members arrived home from work or vacation.

"Rosie, is that you honey?" Ms. Daisy yelled from her bedroom where she watched old Western movies all day.

"Yes, Ms. Daisy, good afternoon. You look beautiful, are you going on a date?" Rosie said kissing her forehead which was warm as she laid on her bed in her diaper full of shit and piss.

Ms. Daisy was a seventy-two-year-old black woman, a retired travel agent with two sons who looked after her, but she was a handful. She needed help to bathe, use the bathroom, eat, and walk around. She was overweight and her old bones couldn't take the weight without her walking on a walker or in a wheelchair.

"Save it—you must have had a sex date since you are thirty minutes late again," Ms. Daisy said, raising her thick eyebrows at her.

"Excuse me—" Rosie started with a chuckle.

"You heard me loud and clear, young lady, now pass me a cigarette and I think I have to use the bathroom."

"You think?" Rosie handed her a cigarette, trying not to vomit as usual. Rosie escorted her to the bathroom, bath her, cooked, cleaned, and did whatever she asked for seven hours per her everyday routine, but Ms. Daisy wasn't her worst client.

Lamaran Street, O-Block

Kip walked down an alley behind homes to meet with his ride-or-die chick Miranda who was a bad, young bitch he never got to fuck but tonight was supposed to be the night that it goes down and he was thirsty.

Kip was a twenty-year-old hustler from Chapell Street a cape four blocks away from where the GDs hustled. Kip was a GD and being on a BD block wasn't smart because the two have been rivals since the 80s, but Kip knew everybody on O-Block and didn't have problems with nobody. He had to sneak through the back because it was close to midnight and O-Block niggas were known for catching niggas looking on the block at night. Kip wore a Balmain top and bottom outfit with a WS Cuban link chain and a Submariner Rolex watch on his wrist stuntin'. Miranda lived four houses down his dick got harder knowing he was about to tear some pussy up.

A man hopped out from behind a fence in front of Kip with a gun to his face that had a long 30 shot clip.

"Man, please I'll turn around and leave. I thought I was on Paxton Street," Kip said as his heart raced.

"Shut up, Joe. What you got in your pockets?" the man said patting him down, feeling two wads of money in his pocket. "Oh, jackpot, pull it out, Moe."

Kip did as he was told and handed the man the $3700 he made throughout the day that he was going to show off in front of Miranda so she could hop on his dick with ease.

"Give me this chain and watch." He robbed Kip of everything.

He fought hard not to cry as tears welled in his eyes. When the light hit the gunman's face a little Kip knew who the man was because they'd gone to middle school together and he knew his big frame looked familiar.

"DeWayne, you Animal? It's me, Kip."

Animal knew very well who the Kip was, but he could care less he needed a lick and it just so happens that Kip's goofy ass was the first nigga to walk through the back alley.

"You got the wrong nigga, Joe. Now get going."

20

"We went to middle school together, Joe. You gonna do me like this?" Kip said as Animal shook his head trying to give him a way out.

Boc! Boc! Boc! Boc! Boc! Boc! Bullets entered Kip's face and his body collapsed into a pile of dirt and trash behind Miranda's house.

Animal drugged his dead body near a trash can, as dogs started to bark. "A dead man doesn't need shoes to walk. This ain't the walking dead nigga!" Animal said loudly as he took Kip's Balmain shoes off his lifeless feet then dashed down the alley cutting through two yards until he made it home.

Romell Tukes

Chapter 3

Harvey, IL

Malik exited his job at a metal cutting factory forty-five minutes outside of Chicago. The job was the only thing paying the bills at him and his girlfriend's crib. He took a smoke break thinking about an employee he cursed out earlier for trying to direct him on how to do his job which he did perfectly. Malik had been working here for the last year since he was fired from Best Buy because he beat up the manager. Malik was from 87th and Jeffery Street, a circle in Chicago besides the Mafia and little street gangs from the 1920s. He was also a CVL Vice Lord just like his stepdad and family members for years.

Being twenty-years-old in Chi-Raq was a blessing because most niggas ain't make it to sixteen so he treasured being twenty and with two bodies under his belt he was humble and laid back. The only friends he had were Boss and Animal other than that he normally stayed to himself because he couldn't trust a soul in the streets. Everybody was void and the one a man trusted the most would murder him the fastest.

Malik was s real nigga with shoulder-length dreads, six-foot-tall, skinny with big lips. He had a five o'clock shadow, tats all over his body, and his name tatted above his left eyebrow. His father had been killed days after he was born by the Black P Stones in a gang war and his mother was left to raise him alone. His mother Roxy found a new man named Steven, she ended up marrying him and having a beautiful daughter named Jasmine a year after Malik's father's death. Steven basically raised Malik into a man, Malik had respect for him because he always treated his mom with the utmost respect.

Checking his G-Shock watch he realized he had five minutes left to go back inside the toxic factory where you had to wear a mask and eventually one could catch cancer. Malik needed a new job because he and his girlfriend Simone were late on bills and that made their relationships bitter.

As soon as he walked inside the busy factory, he saw his boss, an older Uncle Tom black man. "Malik Fielder, may I see you in my office?

'It's *Fields*."

"Oh, okay," the uptight black man said, walking into his office in the back.

Inside the old-fashioned office with old fashion carpeting wall-paper and furniture. Malik thought his boss wanted to be white so bad he even married a white woman.

"Mr. Fields, I received a report today of you threatening one of my staff. Is this true?"

"I'm unaware of this boss man," Malik said, stroking his ego and calling him boss man because he knew Uncle Tom's loved to be called Bossman.

"Save the *boss man* shit this is the third confirmation you have had since you've been here. I'm trying not to be an asshole, but your actions only lead me to one thing."

"Hold on Mr. Johnson, I'm one of the best workers you have. Whenever you need me to fill in for someone, I'm here. I'm never late, and I do my job. To let me go wouldn't be fair over bullshit," Malik said trying to save his job.

"For us, Malik life isn't fair. I'm sorry you're fired. I wish you well." Mr. Jackson put on his glasses and started typing in his old-fashioned Dell computer, taking him off the payroll.

"There no us you're the worst type of cracker, my nigga. I better not catch you in Chicago nigga. Suck my dick!" Malik yelled, knocking the man's papers, computer, and photos off his desk.

Mr. Johnson got scared and was getting ready to call the police when Malik snatched the phone cord out of the wall.

"I should choke you out with this but you're not worth it," Malik said before leaving his office pissed off he'd just lost a good-paying job.

Wentworth Street

Uncle Jay was his name and any hustle was his game, he was Boss under his father's brother but he had a different type of blood running through his poisonous veins. He'd been a drug addict since he was a teenager, he was a smack user who sniffed dope but looked down on people who shot dope in their veins. While his brother who was Boss's father was in the streets killing and robbing shit, sniffing dope, and pimpin' bitches to get his next hit.

Uncle Jay was forty-three-years old he was the old school, pimp nigga type, a smooth talker, and a puppet master. Uncle Jay found himself in a big mess. He owed most of the big-time drug dealers a lot of money and they wanted his head. He had two white bitches selling pussy for him but one of them recently got arrested and the one who was his bottom bitch was only good for sucking dick because her pussy had a bad odor and would run the John's away.

Uncle Jay had to come up with a plan quickly because he was too old to kill half the city. He knew one person who could, but he didn't have the money to buy his services. Plus, he still owed him money. Like a lightbulb, an idea went off in his head. He came up with a grand plan, but it was about putting it together where nobody could see his true agenda.

Uncle Jay smiled, showing his rotten, dirty teeth as he looked at the crackhead, redhead, petite, white chick laying on the floor in the corner.

He took his rolled dollar bill and took a hit off the tan substance. "Ahhh," he moaned as the dope hit his veins. He yelled for Amber to wake up. "Come suck this dick," he said pulling his dick out of his boxers as she got between his legs, wiping the crust out her eyes as she went to work.

Amber deep throated his dick, working her way up and down making loud, noisy sucking sounds. She deep throated his big click in one motion until he came in her mouth. Once she swallowed him, she was horny and ready to get fucked in her ass until he told her to go back to sleep and get ready to hit the track hard that night.

Uncle Jay was a Black P Stone like his brother who was a big homie but he had no rank whatsoever because he was a dopehead and he did a lot of shady shit to his homies the only reason he wasn't dead was because of his brother.

Buff City

Lil BD was posted on the block with his crew of young niggas with pipes everywhere throughout the block. Buff City was a notorious Black Disciple area ran from the 100s to 119[th,] if a nigga wasn't BD he wasn't coming through Buff City unless he was someone in power. Lil BD was Boss' little brother; he was a Black Disciple, nineteen-years-old, a high school graduate, and a very smart kid. He was a mama's boy but loved the street life. He looked just like Boss except he had waves and was shorter. His father became a junkie after spending seventeen years in the Marines.

When he would see his father across town in the far corner Hustler area, he would walk right past him. One day his father even asked him if he had some drugs unaware that Lil BD was his son because he had not seen him since he was two years old before he went off to the Marines.

"Lil BD, them two bitches pulling up. They valid and they both eaters and Hitler said he can his way," Curtis said coming out of the kick spot for the young BDs.

"A'ight, Joe," Lil BD said, texting his best friend Hitler a four-corner hustler member but he was good everywhere.

Chapter 4

South Side Chicago: Riverside High School

"Who can tell me the year Illinois became a state?" Ms. Johnson asked her summer school History class.

"eighteen-eighteen," a student replied before raising her hand.

"Okay, the constitution banned slavery that year but what was allowed?" Ms. Johnson asked her class standing at the front desk.

"Indentured servitude for twenty-five years," a fat 8th-grade student stated sitting in the back.

"Correct, Mr. Richardson. Back then Blacks had no rights as citizens. We couldn't serve on juries, either. Who knows when this time changed?"

"After the civil war in eighteen-seventy-four that's when blacks could finally vote and attend school with Whites," one of her smartest students stated who was only in summer school for extra credit and to help other students.

"Great you are all so smart, but class is over. Enjoy the weekend, be safe and please do all of your homework, class dismissed." Ms. Johnson sat down at her desk as students rushed out of her history class at 1:00 pm. Summer school was over at 1 p.m. Monday-Friday for kids who needed credits to pass to the next grade.

Ms. Johnson was a beautiful, flawless, caramel-skinned woman, she had long, neat, perfect dreads to show her deep Haitian roots, she had bright hazel eyes and a sexy body no man would ever turn down. For forty-years-old, she was eye candy but she carried herself as a real woman with respect and honor. She was the mother of Boss and Lil BD. She did her best raising two boys on her own. Since Boss's dad was serving a life sentence and Lil BD's dad was a junkie she had no choice but to be a mother and a father. Living in Chicago especially on the Southside kids had an 87% chance of being involved in gang activity. Growing up she was a Black Panther but as she grew older, she became just for her people, teaching the youth about their history and why they should never take it for granted.

Her children were very intelligent; they'd just made the wrong choices, but she understood a man for his ups and downs. Janella Johnson grabbed her big purse and made her way to the teacher's car lot. She was drained being an 8th-grade History teacher was harder than anyone could imagine. Once outside she bumped into a middle-aged teacher who was tall and handsome but fucked almost every teacher in the school, including the married ones. He was dark, nicely built, with a nice smile.

"Ms. Johnson, how are you doing? I haven't seen you in days," he said chasing her down in the parking lot looking at her ample, heart-shaped ass in her pencil skirt.

"I've been working with Mr. Lawrence. How may I help you?" she replied as she stepped out of her black Range Rover sport truck shitting on his eight-year-old Honda parked four cars over.

"I just wanted to say hi and see if one day we could go out for a bite to eat and drink?" he said.

Her face turned over. "I don't go on dates with co-workers and you're not my type, no disrespect. I'm a little out of your league," she said.

He looked into her hazel, sexy eyes. "Okay, uhhhh, hope to see you around then," he said walking off toward a new Mercedes Benz acting like it was his while digging in his pockets as if he'd lost his keys aware that she was watching. "Okay, I forgot my keys inside," he said walking back towards the building.

"I'm sure the principal can help you find the keys to his car." She saw the craziest look on his face as if he was a kid caught doing something wrong, Janelle hopped in her Range and pulled out the lot.

Buff City

Animal walked down the street in a new Nike tracksuit, with a pair of running shoes on, on his way to run some laps at the race-track across the street from a middle school. Since he'd robbed Kip, he was laying low because the block was hot. It was the first body of the summer and the GDs were pissed and ready to take action on

28

the BDs but they had no clue who'd killed their homie. This was Animal's first time out during the day. He had to get some air because his mom and sister were driving him crazy for rent money, food, drug money, and clothes. Once they saw him with a new pair of shoes, they knew he was up to no good so they were going to use him up until he went back to jail again.

Animal felt the Chicago heat he loved as he watched females walking around with their asses hanging out. He was supposed to meet up with a bitch from 75th and Ellis tonight that he met on his social media page. As he started walking a gray BME 18 pulled up on him with tints. Animal had the same gun on him he'd used to kill Kip and wouldn't hesitate to shoot whoever was pulling up on him because the city was full of cops,

The tinted windows rolled down. "What's up, BD?" Loso yelled out of his lowered window. He was iced out in jewelry with a big Jesus piece and a six-point star behind it and a big faced Rolex watch with diamonds all through the face.

"Damn, bro this shit 'void.'"

"Get in, spin the block with me," Loso said and Animal climbed inside the deep leather seats.

Loso was Animal's big homie and most every BD's big homie in Bluff City. He had a lot of pull and ties in the city. He was only thirty-two years old and already a stamped OG in the city. He was moving at least eight keys every other day.

"Good to see you, homie."

"Yeah, thank you. Welcome home, the guys told me you were behind the wall holding your own as we do," Loso said, stopping at a red light to see everybody admiring his car as if he was Kanye West coming back to the hood which was unheard of.

"That's what's up, Joe. I was fucking with the guys and on my exercise shit."

"I see you got big as a house. But what's your plan now that you're home? I know you trying to get some money."

"Facts, I'm sick of being fucked up and broke. I'm trying to run it up, and get me one of these bad boys, Joe," Animal said, making Loso laugh.

"Yeah, homie this is a year of hard work but I'ma put you on your feet, right now," Loso said.

Loso pulled out a small sandwich bag from his pocket with a couple of pieces of chunked cake inside and handed it to Animal. Loso then pulled out a wad of hundred blue faces that were close to 30K and handed Animal one bill which was a hundred dollars.

Animal still had his hand out as if he wasn't done but when Loso gave him a crazy look with wide eyes, Animal just placed the work and money in his pockets.

"That's an eight ball of crack. You should be good, welcome home. Tell NaNa I said hi," Loso said referring to his sister who he used to fuck years ago before she became a thot and got washed up.

"A'ight, good lookin' I'ma get up with you."

"Do that, Joe. Shit getting crazy out here. Niggas killed a nigga a couple of nights ago and niggas went to set up a meeting. So, I gotta go holler at Shooter and 'em niggas but be safe."

"Always." Animal walked off. He was pissed that his big homie just played him by giving him an 8 ball and he was a bricklayer.

Chapter 5

Hazelton USP, WV

Tyrell Sr. a.k.a Ty Stone was in a West Virginia federal maximum-security prison in the mountains, hours away from Chicago. Ty Stone had been locked up for nineteen years now for drugs, violence, and gang activity. He was Boss's father even though he was locked up his whole life the two were able to build a good relationship as Boss got older. Coming to prison at twenty years old was enough because his whole life was snatched from under his feet.

When the judge sentenced him to life in federal prison he felt as if someone punched the soul from his heart. Most of his co-defendants snitched on him which was another low blow because these were his day one niggas and niggas he grew up with. Growing up in the 100s block around the Black P Stones Rangers only turned him into one of the most dangerous P Stones in the city. Before he caught his case, he was the gang's main connect.

While in prison Ty Stone used his time wisely studying how to get back in court on an appeal motion. He became a Muslim as most Stones were anyway. He exercised five days a week, prayed, stayed to himself, and sold drugs in the prison to maintain, even though he had financial support. He hated calling home for money as most inmates would do every day driving their families crazy. Prison behind the wall in a maximum-security prison wasn't easy. There was so much going on and niggas were dying every day. Snitches were coming off the bus to get beat up or stabbed and niggas were stealing from each other.

Different states and gangs were crushing each other and then it was the crazy race riots where blacks had to stick together to push a hard line, against other races but most blocks could run and hide in the cell.

"Ty Stone, what's up? I ain't seen you in months, Slim. Where you been?" his man Lee from D.C. said as they were walking to the library together on the packed walkway with inmates dressed in tan uniforms.

"We were on lockdown for two months, Joe. After them New York niggas crashed out with the South over there in A-2 unit," Ty stone said as a couple of inmates walked past him nodding their heads.

"I heard about that, Slim. But I got my appeal back," Lee said. "What happened?"

"Man, they denied me, Slim. That was my last one, my only hope, Slim. I'm going on twenty-seven years in the belly of the beast," Lee said shaking his head as they entered the school building.

"Sorry to hear that but don't give up. They got a gang of new laws coming out next year. Have faith and trust in Allah."

"Facts, I'ma go holler at this nigga Double O. I'ma get up with you later, Slim," Lee said walking off.

Ty Stone continued into the library. Ty Stone still looked the same way he did when he came in at twenty, now he was thirty-nine years old. Eating clean was a big part of his limitless aging. No pork, no red meat, no drug use, and he tried his best not to stress which was hard when a nigga didn't have an out date.

He was tall, chiseled, brown-skinned, clean out, with low Caesar cut, handsome, had a professional appearance, and carried himself with respect. He was the big homie of the P Stones and throughout all the federal prisons he called the hits and controlled the gang behind the wall.

Buff City, Southside

"Don't leave a crumb," Loso said as he walked around the apartment he usually worked in.

He had six young workers in the living room at table stations, bussing down bricks and bagging them up into ounces, 8 balls, and 3 ½ grams.

"Weigh every key before you cut it open, Joe. If that shit don't say one-thousand-eight grams don't touch it," Loso instructed, watching his gang and workers as if they were in a sweatshop in Mexico City.

Loso's plug was a Latin King who he'd been dealing with for over seven years now. He had good product and one of the best prices in the town. Loso had the trade in Bluff City on since the real Buff died years ago. Now Loso was the new leader in charge, he was the number one BD in charge of the city.

He ran the 100s to 119th, Dirty Hairy, and O-Block, the motherland for the BDs, and the O.T.F. crew who fucked with Loso hard. Last week Loso bought a nice house on the outskirts of the city in Harey, IL for his mom who he loved dearly and took care of even though she was a hot mess. This morning Loso re-upped thirty-five keys before it was almost the first of the month and the twins in Bluff City spent big, so he wanted to be ready.

Loso's right-hand man and the second general of the BDs were coming home in a couple of weeks. His man Fame just did ten years in the feds and he wanted him to come home to a nice luxury car and a big bag.

Southside

Boss drove through Perry Street to see that the hood was out and posted up on the stoop smoking, drinking, shooting dice, and enjoying the hot summer day. Boss had an all-black BMW M5 with tints, it was clean and a head turner but it was nothing compared to what the major niggas were driving around in. Last night his Uncle Jay called him and told him he needed to speak to him asap about something important and he agreed.

The last time Boss saw his uncle was at his Aunty Lisa's funeral after she died from a stroke at the nursing home where she was living because she was old and sick. He didn't really fuck with his Uncle like that because when he needed a father figure growing up Jay was nowhere in sight and Boss believed in family first.

Boss knew his Uncle Jay was a washed-up pimp with a dope habit, that wasn't hard to tell when one saw his appearance in his old thrift store, suit, and attire. As he pulled up to the old run-down building which was the address he gave him last night. Boss saw hackers and veins running up and down the block in the summer heat. Boss walked into the dirty building, up the stairs to the second floor, and apartment 2B. He knocked and a white woman answered the door. She had yellow teeth and looked to be in her early 30s with a cute face and petite body, but you could tell she was a hard drug user.

He saw her nipple poking out of her dirty, tan top and her big pussy budging in her pink, baggy shorts.

"Hey," she said, licking her lips and crossing her little dirty feet ready to suck his dick as she stared down at his Gucci shorts, shirt, and sneakers.

"Let him in!" a voice yelled from inside.

"Okay, daddy!" she yelled. "Come on, please. I have a deep throat like no other. I would love to taste your cum, big daddy," she whispered to Boss as he walked in.

"I'm good," Boss replied, smelling the funk from her mouth.

"Nephew, come here. You gotta hit that track bitch and put on some heels. I know you see all that money out here," Uncle Jay snapped at his main hoe.

"Yes, daddy," she said as she put on some heels as rushed out of the dirty apartment.

"Have a seat. That BMW clean youngin," Uncle Jay said.

Boss looked around the junky, dirty, smelly apartment and chose to stand up. "I'll stand. But what's up?"

"Straight to the point I see," Uncle Jay said dressed in a cotton green robe and slippers. "Okay, look I know you move your little weed and shit nephew, but that's chump change. I know how to get you big money."

"Talk I'm all ears."

"Okay, I know a lot of heavy hitters in the city. I'ma put you in line and you just take them out, rob them blind and we eat. But we have to be smart because these are powerful people. If word gets back that we're responsible, the city will come after us."

"What's in it for you?" Boss asked.

"Fifty percent, nigga. I'm getting you a location and the lick," Uncle Jay replied.

"Nigga, do I look dumb? It's twenty-five percent or nothing."

"Thirty-five percent," Uncle Jay challenged.

"Twenty-five or I walk now," Boss said.

"Okay, man damn—deal. Nephew, give me a couple days. I got something lined up. If you use a crew, please get niggas you can trust. Oh, and you don't know me if you get caught."

"I ain't never known you, and I do got a crew."

"Who?"

"Chi' Raq Gangstas."

"Okay, gangsta, I'ma holler at you soon," Uncle Jay said.

As Boss walked out, both men smiled at the thoughts that filled both of their minds with different agendas.

Romell Tukes

Chapter 6

87th and Jeffery

"Malik, you haven't been home in days. That girl called my phone looking for you boy," his mother Roxy said walking into the living room in a robe.

Roxy was a little on the chubby side, but she was still cute and dark with a good spirit. She was a full-blown church woman now. She worked at a nursing home while her husband Steven worked in construction.

Since he'd lost his job, he'd have been a bump on a log and depressed. Now he either had to find a new job or find a hustle because bills were due in days.

"Baby, you need to get it together. You lost your damn job, not your mind. When one door closes another one always opens," she said walking into the kitchen.

He sucked his teeth not really trying to hear that shit because he knew she wasn't going to pay his bills. He and Simone would be in a shelter somewhere if that was the case.

Malik's sister came downstairs in a sundress with sandals showing her manicured feet and cute toes. Jasmine was a sexy, redbone, thick, with big juicy pink lips, green eyes, big titties, and a sexy catwalk. Everybody in the hood wanted to fuck but she didn't give niggas the time of day because she was focused on going to college and she was only eighteen-years-old.

"Malik you still here? I haven't seen you home this much since your dirty ass moved out," Jasmine said sitting next to her brother.

"Watch your mouth in my damn house!" Roxy yelled from the kitchen.

"I'ma slide to the crib tonight."

"You going to take me to work so I don't have to call an uber?"

"Nigga, you got gas money?"

"Yeah, you broke ass nigga," she said handing him twenty dollars out of her fake Louis Vuitton purse.

"Jasmine!" her mother yelled.

"I'm sorry, ma. We are leaving!" Jasmine shouted as she and Malik left the house and hoped in his Kia Stinger he leased.

"Where you work at again?" he asked, pulling off the block to see Vice Lords on every corner early in the morning.

"Nigga, you know I work at the daycare on Clyde Street," she said turning up the new King Van song on the radio.

Malik saw he had a text from Boss on his phone as he stopped at a red light. The text said: *//: Hit me ASAP!* This made him smile because he had a feeling it was time.

Later That Night

The crew met across town near the Cook County jail in a Latin King's hood made of a small park that was dark and empty.

"Welcome home, bro. How come you ain't hit the guys, Joe? You know we would have set you out," Boss told Animal who'd gotten big ass a house.

"I had to get my mind right and get focus first. You know, I had to get used to society again. You know y'all did enough for me already. I love y'all niggas I ain't miss a commissary," Animal stated seriously as they stood in a small circle.

"We family, bro, loyalty is openly viewed in hard times and good times," Malik said speaking from the heart.

"Facts, but tonight we will embark on our journey as the Chi'Raq Gangstas, it's time we take what's ours—the city. I'ma be real we're going to lose a lot of blood and gain a lot of pain in the process of trying to get to the top so if anyone of you not ready then walk away," Boss said

"I'm in it until my casket drops. This is all I know," Malik said.

"A'ight good. Since that's established it's time we discuss our new way of living. My Uncle knows all the heavy hitters in the city and on the outskirts. So, he's going to plug me in on who is doing what," Boss left out the big issues that would make most think twice because doing anything with a dopehead was a No-No in Chi'Raq.

"Can we trust him?" Animal asked.

"We're gonna have to and if we see any shit that doesn't sit right then we abort the mission," Boss said.

"What we gonna do if any of our vias backfire? Because you knew karma is a bitch," Malik said.

"Yeah, what if niggas find out we them niggas that's been crushing shit in the city?" Animal asked.

"Then we go turn the fuck up. Malik, you still got the gun connect?" Boss asked.

"Yep," Malik said referring to his cousin who was in the army. He'd steal bags of guns and then sell them to his people.

"Okay, perfect. When my uncle gives us our first vic, I'll holler at y'all. We only meet at night in the park to discuss business. I think we should not bring anybody to our table unless needed," Boss said.

"I agree," Animal said.

"Me too," Malik added

"Until then I got a via for us," Animal said as the crowd looked at him. "His name is Loso."

"Hold on that's your big homie," Boss said laughing.

"Anybody can get it," Malik added.

"No question but he's up big time. Just give me a couple of days. I'll have a location and we can do our thing ski-masked the fast way," Animal said getting everybody excited.

"A'ight so we wait on Animal's call until then Malik holler at your people. Tell them I got a couple of Dracos, 5Ks, and ARs," Boss stated.

"Say no more, Joe," Malik said.

The men talked for another twenty minutes before they all split up and went separate ways with money on their minds.

Downtown Chicago

Animal was working out in a gym filled with men and women of all ages and races exercising trying to stay fit for the summer. He was lifting 100-pound dumbbells and doing butterflies with them with ease for eight sets. Other fitness junkies eyed him, sizing him up, wondering if he juiced in order to blow up the way he did. Animal used exercise as a stress reliever, and it helped him get his thought process together. Robbing Loso was the decision he'd made the day he gave him an 8 ball and a punk-ass 100-dollar bill as if he was just a little nigga penny-pinching.

As he was working out, he saw a sexy, light-brown-skinned chick approaching him in exercise gear with her long hair in a bun.

"BD, what's up?" the woman said, throwing up the BD gang sign. He threw it back up trying to remember who she was. "Damn, nigga you ain't been gone that long. Jenny, I live a couple of houses down from you, nigga. You basically raised me," she said.

Now he knew who she was, but her body had blossomed fast. "Oh, shit," he said, trying not to stare at her crazy, perfectly, curve body.

Jenny was nineteen-years-old, in college, a BD chick from O-Block and she was beautiful. One wouldn't imagine she was a gang-banger. She was 5'7, with light-brown, almond-shaped eyes, a clean flawless face, flat abs, nice C-cup perky boobs, a round nice soft ass, curvy, long, legs, and long natural hair because she had Indian in her blood.

"You got so big I ain't even know that was you."

"I'm done now. You about to leave?"

"Yeah," she said smiling.

"A'ight," he said.

"What you been up to? What you got going on for yourself? I know it's hard coming home. So, if you need anything, I got you. The guys be on some goofy shit, I don't fuck with none of them niggas," she said stopping at her navy-blue Infiniti Q60 with rims and tints.

"I already know how the gang be moving but I do need a favor. You know Loso, right?"

"Yeah, I know the so-called big homie. The only reason why niggas fucking with him is because he's feeding the wolves," she said leaning on her car.

"You know where he lives?" he asked straight up.

Chi'Raq Gangstas

She looked at him as if he was crazy. "Nigga, you not about to get me indicted, I don't speak tongue," she said rolling her neck. "And I know what type of time you on. I saw you that night Kip got wet up. You ran through my backyard like your ol' big ass could get low," she said laughing.

Jenny was a street bitch, she killed, robbed, and sold drugs. She saw it all, she'd lost a lot of family members and guys to the streets. Her mother and uncles raised her once her dad was nowhere to be found. She'd never even met the man but her mom Ashely did a good job. Jenny went to college, work, and scammed on the side.

"Please I'll pay you, I need you but this between us."

"I have a friend that he's fucking so I'll squeeze some shit out of her and you better come right when you have my money. Don't let my looks fool you, nigga. All that big shit don't scare me. You need a ride?" she said laughing but she was so serious.

"Nah, I'm good. I'ma grab a bite to eat."

"Okay. Oh, and by the way your Rolex is fake. Real Rolexes tick clockwise with no noise. So, get your money back." She got in her car laughing hard as hell.

Animal listened to his watch he'd taken from Kip ticking loudly.

Romell Tukes

Chapter 7

"Ummmm ahhhhh!" Simone yelled as she wrapped one leg around Malik's waist as he slowly shoved his pole in and out of the small, pussy that was dripping wet.

Simone closed her eyes, the dick was so good, and the pleasure and pain made her want to scream his name like a church chorus harmony. Malik lifted her other leg over his shoulder and reigned deeper as she braced herself.

He started sucking on her toes.

"Ooooohhhh!" she screamed as her body went into spasms, he was hitting her spot. "I'm-m-m-m cumming!" she yelled as her juices covered his dick. Malik's face tightened as he nutted inside of her. "Yessss—cum in this pussy," she moaned, feeling her pussy fill with thick cum. When he finally pulled out, creamy cum was flowing at the small slit of her perfect, bald, phat pussy.

"Turn over, baby," he demanded.

She laid flat on her stomach, tooted her phat ass in the sky, and spread her ass cheeks so she could feel all of 8 ½ inches.

"Ooohhh awwww fuck me, daddy!" she screamed as he slowly pounded her back out making her ass clap.

He slid in and out her wetness as her pussy walls grabbed his dick. "Say my name, bitch."

"Malik!"

"Louder, bitch," he said, grabbing a handful of her hair.

"Malik!" she yelled at the top of her lungs as she climaxed feeling as if she was in paradise.

Once they both came Simone climbed on his dick with ease, her big breasts flapped up and down as she raised and came crashing down on his dick, rotating her hips.

"Shiiiit—you like that?" she said biting her lips and bouncing her ass everywhere like waves and dropping low on his dick while grinding until he couldn't take no more.

"I'm cuummiiinnngggg!" he yelled.

Simone hopped off his dick and swallowed him whole as she worked her thin lips around the head of his dick. He thrust in her mouth and she allowed him to bang the back of her throat out. He grabbed the back of her head and forced her head down as she let him shoot off in her throat, she gulped every drop.

"Damn," he said because sex hadn't been this good in months.

"Happy Anniversary, baby," she said looking at the clock seeing that it was time for her to go to work at Family Dollar where she was a clerk/cashier.

"I love you," he said, looking at her big, yellow ass strut to the bathroom.

"Love you more. Get dressed so you can take me to work," Simone said as she entered the bathroom.

Simone was a masterpiece of beauty, her mother was white, and her father was black as night but they were from Pretoria South Africa. She came to Chicago when she was three-years-old, now she was twenty-one.

She was so yellow most people thought she was white, plus she had bright, blue eyes. She was super thick with double DD breasts and shoulder-length, curly, dark hair. She modeled for two magazines, but she was shy and had respect for herself.

The couple had been together for five years today and they had moved in together two years ago. She worked as a cashier and since Malik lost his job, she was holding it down which she didn't mind because they were a team.

Malik had to do something quick. They hoped that Animal's plan would come any day now because he didn't even have gas money.

Michigan Ave Mall

Jenny and her friend Kimberly a.k.a Kimmie were shopping in the mall located two minutes outside of a city. They were in the Versace store looking at purses, dresses, and shoes.

44

"How's school, girl? I can't believe you got into a University. Girl, I can't even pass the test to get in a community college," Kimme said, making Jenny laugh.

"Oh, yeah, I forgot when we were in high school. You were in the special class with the kid who drooled all day and the fat kid who used to bang his head on everybody's locker," Jenny said laughing.

"Don't remind me but that fat kid was killed by police over there on Langley Street. They knew that boy was fucked up in the head," Kimme said watching two dudes stare at her crazy ass sitting on her back.

Kimme was a regular, cute, dark-skinned hood rat, but last year she went to DR to get her ass done, and now she was the talk of the town plus working in Sky II, Red Diamond, and The Factory she was the hottest stripper in the city.

"What's good in these strip clubs? I know you are twerking that big old ass," Jenny said twerking in her hands as her ass bounced while shoppers stared because Jenny was a bad bitch.

"Yeah, girl, I am getting a check. I just copped a Benz truck last week," Kimmie said.

"Yeah, I saw you climb out of it. I was like bitch okay, I gotta step my shit up."

"My side nigga did that, side bitches is winning period," Kimmie said laughing.

"You ain't never lied. You still fucking with, Loso?" Jenny asked, looking at a Bersoca two-piece dress.

"Yeah, this nigga got me pregnant, girl. I told him if he doesn't get me a Benz truck, I was keeping it. The next day we were at the car lot," she explained laughing.

"Bitch you grimy."

"Shit that nigga just bought a nice house in Harvey, Illinois on Carria Street where all them nice cribs at. He got a three-car garage. I fucked him all over that house last night after the club while his mom was there you know he's a mama boy."

45

"That's what's up. I've been fucking with this nigga named, Frank. He plays ball overseas. He's a little old at twenty-seven but he is fire, bitch," Jenny said thinking about her boo.

"Okay, I see you," Kimmie said as they continued shopping and have a girl day out while over forty niggas tried to holla at them and they curved all of them.

Later

Jenny was in the dark park running laps at 9:45 p.m. as she did daily to beat the hot summer heat. She was waiting on Animal so she could give him the 411 on Loso and so she could get paid. She could give a fuck less about Loso or really no nigga, she was about her bag. She finally saw Animal walk through the gate in a Nike running suit

"L's up." Animal acknowledged her with their Lamaran Street greeting.

"Always! Take a lap with me," she said seeing that he'd taken off his fake Rolex.

"What's the drill?" Animal said looking at her sexy, feathers and long hair in a bun, he thought about trying to holler at her to get in her panties but thought better of it despite the fact that her sex appeal was crazy strong.

"Loso got a new house in Harvey, Illinois on Carner Street. He got an Audi, a BMW truck, and a motorcycle, I always see him on," she said.

"Good, thank you."

"Nigga, fuck thank you, pay me," she said holding out her hand with her other hand on her hips.

"I'll get up with you in a few days, trust me," he said, turning to leave so he could get up with the guys and put their plan in motion.

Jenny shook her head and continued running the track and listening to her iPod. She trusted Animal enough for him not to play with her money and if he did, she had no issue smoking his ass, he wouldn't be her first body. Two years ago, she met with a nigga to chill. He tried to rape her, and she shot him six times in the head in the hotel and got away with it.

Last year she killed a GD nigga for slapping her outside his crib after an argument because she did some scamming for him and he was supposed to bust down the money 50/50 but instead he took it all and slapped her. Hours later she came back with a ski mask and gloves and killed him in the same spot he'd slapped her. Most people would think she was just a sexy model bitch, but she was a different type of savage.

Romell Tukes

Chapter 8

Harvey, IL

"Nigga we been out here on this dark ass block for three hours watching this brick house to only see an old bitch walking back and forth," Malik said. "Are you sure this is the right address, bro?" Malik looked at Animal who was in the back seat of the stolen Mazda.

"It's only twelve-thirty give it some same time, but this is it trust me," Animal said looking at the three-car garage home.

"You never want to be in a hurry because hurrying portrays a lack of control over yourself and over time, bro. So, always seem patient as if you know everything will come to you eventually," Boss said sitting in the driver's seat.

"Well, as Napoleon used to say we can never recover time," Malik said.

"It's all about waiting patiently for the right moment to act, putting competitors off their front by messing with their time. Patience is like a snake it calms with a seedy flow then boom it strikes," Animal added laughing.

"Well, it's time to strike," the boss said, seeing a pair of HD lights speed down the quiet block as the engine roared.

"About time, I was starting to doubt you, big boy," Malik said seeing the Audi swerve into the first open garage which opened and closed and had another car parked inside.

"We stick to the plan in and out, Joe. Quiet as a church mouse," Boss instructed, placing a silencer over his Glock and a ski mask on his face, his crew did the same.

Loso was coming from a party in a new club in downtown Chicago he'd brought his crew out and they shut the club down.

"Ma, what's up? Why you still up?" Loso said still feeling tipsy from drinking all night.

"Boy, I'm grown. Two of your baby mothers called me looking for you because they say your phone was off. Them bitches want some money. I told you to never claim them little bastards," his mama said, standing in the kitchen warming up leftover fried fish from last night.

His mother was an old, evil, gray hair bitch. She was into females after she had Loso and his father gave her HIV but she never told Loso he was born with HIV and she was glad he never got tested, but she felt sad for his bitches because there was a big chance they had the virus.

"I'm tired," he said, sitting at his dining room table, unaware how late it was as he closed his eyes.

Seconds later, he thought he heard something. He saw his mama walk into the dining room with her hands in the air to be followed by three mask men with guns. Loso got nervous he'd left his gun in his car, something he never did and now he regretted it.

"Put your hands up, nigga!" Boss yelled to Loso as his man pushed him in a chair next to him.

"Where the shit at?" Malik asked.

"We don't know what you talkin' about. This is the house of the Lord," his mama said even though she'd never stepped foot inside a church, and she didn't believe in the Lord.

Boss laughed and shot her in her thigh causing her to yell out in pain.

"Okay, please don't hurt her. I have nothing here except twenty-K under the couch. My stash house is on Dorchester Street in the city, please," he begged.

All three men looked at each other. "I'm going! What's the addy, Joe?" Malik asked as he took the keys off the table.

"Five-ninety-seven Dorchester, apartment three S. Everything is in the hall closet," Loso said.

Malik knew where the place was by heart as he left. Animal and Boss sat down holding the two at gunpoint and finally they took off their masks.

"You dirty motherfucker," Loso said with fire in his eyes when he saw Animal and the other nigga with dreads who he'd never seen before.

50

"Payback's a bitch. You remember that eight ball you gave me? You cheap-ass nigga. That's how you do the guys? Treat us like shit, now it's my time," Animal said smiling.

"The city ain't gonna let you get away with this, Joe. All you niggas dead. You know who the fuck I am!" he shouted.

Both men laughed as they waited to hear back from Malik. Thirty Minutes later Malik called telling him he was on his way back and it was a jackpot.

"Well, everything checked out, Joe. So, thank you for your time. Animal go get that twenty-K from the couch," Boss said as he saw Loso and his mama ice grilling him.

"You can leave now," Loso's mama said to the gangstas, she had a towel tied around her thigh to stop the bleeding.

"A'ight, bro, we goo.," Animal smiled, carrying a bag in his hand.Loso mumbled something under his breath.

"Tag team," Boss said.

Animal nodded and fired thirteen rounds into Loso's soul as Boss shot his mama in the head seven times which was his lucky number. Malik pulled up outside minutes later, then they made their way back to town and dumped the car, then made their way to Boss' crib since his girl was at her family's house.

One Week Later

Boss was on his way upstairs to his mom's apartment to bring her some money and check on his little brother who was never home.

"Tyrell, As-salaam-alaikum," a Muslim man said as he opened the door stepping out of his apartment to see his neighbor who he'd watched transform into a man.

"Wa Alaikum Salaam," Boss replied even though he wasn't a Muslim he showed Imam Abu Sa'id respect. He was one of the city's most official gangstas and one of the main Vice Lord members in the 60s.

Let me speak to you youngin'," Imam Sa'id said walking into his clean carpeted apartment as Boss followed him, taking off his shoes as he always did, smelling incenses and Muslim oil.

The apartment smelled of incense and Muslim oils and looked like a Mosque that was filled with Islamic books, DVDs, Oils, Garments, and rugs.

"How are you doing?"

"I'm okay, I just want to speak to you because I basically raised your father and I watched you grow up. A king respects himself and inspires the same sentiment in others. Let your integrity itself be your own standard of rectitude. You're very advanced for a man your age, Tyrell, just as I am," he said rubbing his long, gray beard and looking at Boss with his odd eyes, like a mirror.

"I heard back in your day you had nothing to fool with," Boss said.

"I was, but back in the fifties, sixties, and seventies it was different, dudes were solid and strong. I built an empire off power. But what I didn't know is that power normally has its own rhythms and patterns. Nowadays you have to be a clever strategist when the greatest danger occurs at the moment of victory," he stated sharply.

Boss listened closely, taking in the knowledge while wondering the true meaning of the conversation because Iman Sa'id was the quick type. Iman Sa'id never came out of his home unless it was to go to the mosque or take his grandbaby to school when she spent the week with him.

"One last thing I recently read from Maphi's life story. He said something very strong, he said men are so simple of mind, and so dominated by their immediate needs that a deceitful man will always find plenty who are ready to be deceived."

"That's deep."

"I gotta pray. Tell your mother I send my salaams. Back in her day kid, she was the strongest Black Panther out here. She stood on what she believed in," Iman added, walking Boss to the door. "I'm here, stop by sometime."

"Okay, no problem. Thank you," Boss said, putting on his shoes walking a couple of doors down to his mom's crib.

O-Block

Animal was in the alley behind Jenny's house waiting on her with a bag in his hand. It was 1:00 a.m. but he'd been laying low lately because the city was going crazy over Loso's murder.

He was feeding most of the BDs, the crew received 270,000 in cash and twenty-one pounds of exotic weed and two keys of coke. The crew agreed not to spend money until shit died down, so they wanted to draw heat to them.

Jenny walked out the back of her home into her backyard in her Louis Vuttion pajamas, an LV headscarf, and her iPhone in her hand. She wondered what the fuck he wanted at 1:00 a.m. which made her conceal a .380 special handgun because she knew how the guys were in her hood shady, grimy, and snakes.

"What nigga? You woke me up," she fussed with an attitude still looking sexy fresh out of bed.

"Damn did you even hit your black ass gums?"

"Boy, please you wish my shit looked like your mouthguard," she said.

He laughed and handed her a brown paper bag.

"What's this?" she said looking into a bag to see a stack of money. "Oh, shit! Wow how much is this?" she said shocked.

"Thirty-thousand."

"Oh, my God. Thank you," she said because she was waiting for him to link up with her, but she didn't expect this much money.

"I told you I had you."

"I heard what happened to Loso. Niggas said his mom's face was unrecognizable but the guys is sick, his funeral is tomorrow," she said smiling.

"I know I'll be there to pay my respects and toss a blue face in his casket and an 8 ball. But be easy on spending until shit dies down."

"I look dumb, nigga? I already got a bag, take your own advice, and get a Rolex, big boy," she said walking off.

He watched her ass jiggle. "I just want to taste it," he said to himself before walking off.

Romell Tukes

Chapter 9

75ᵗʰ and Ingleside

Grad Crossings park was packed on Sunday morning with CVL Vice Lords. It was their meeting place and hang out spot. It was a hot summer morning, women were walking around showing off their summer body as niggas posed up chasing, yelling, fighting, smoking, gambling, and blasting music, awaking the whole neighborhood. Malik pulled up in a candy red Shelby, Supersnake Mustang with a roar as a gang of young CVL chicks stood next to a Benz.

Yesterday he traded in his Kia for the new Mustang because of its wide body and 1000hp, he loved fast muscle cars. When he hopped out the gang embraced him, he was a well-known Lord because his step-pop's Steven was one of the high-ranking members in the city.

"Damn, I see you stepping your game up," a sexy, thick, dark-skinned chick said climbing out of a pearl white, Mercedes AMG E63.

"I'm trying, Shayla," he said looking at her phat pussy poking out of her little shorts trying to get air.

Shayla was the Godmother of a CVL, her father started the CVL, and she and her brother in prison were the top dawgs in the city. She was sexy, but a cold-blooded gangsta and twenty-seven-years old. She lived a crazy life and she recently beat a murder wrap.

"That's what's up, I'll see you around," she said climbing in her Mercedes with three other bad bitches.

Malik saw a few of the guys and chilled with them, the lick shit was going great, bills were paid, he had a new car, new clothes, and he put some money up for a rainy day. He wanted to give some money to his mom and sister, but he didn't want them to question him. So, he planned to wait to bless them on his next lick and come up with a story of how he got the bread.

"I don't even see you no more, Joe," Baby Lord remarked sitting on the bench with eight guys.

"Yeah, I been working."

"You stay with a job, but we were beefing with the Latin Disciples over turf. We just killed two guys last night, so just be on point, Lord," Baby Lord warned.

"A'ight, I knew that was going to happen. Our block and their block is connected," said Malik.

"Yeah, but it's about respect and communication. Them niggas think because they moving all that dope they can force their way in our shit. Nah, bro and Shayla was supplying all them niggas until now," B Lord said blowing clouds of weed smoke out of his mouth.

"They know who runs the city."

"No question, Joe." Baby Lord.

Malik chilled with the gang for about an hour then left. As he was on his way to his car, he saw Lil' Rico and his crew getting out of a GMC truck blasting music from LA Capone.

"What's up, cousin?" Malik said as he saw his little cousin high as a kite, walking toward the park.

"Oh, shit. What's good? This you," Lil' Rico said, embracing his older cousin.

Lil' Rico was eighteen-years-old, he was Malik's little cousin on his mom's side, he was a CVL and a troublemaker.

"Yeah, how's the fam?" Malik asked, seeing two CVLs fighting.

"Good everybody great, Joe. I need to get down with you, cuz. Whatever you doing I need to get some money. My girl pregnant, I'm doing bad."

"A'ight, you still got the same number," Malik said digging in his pockets and pulling out 500 dollars, handing it to him.

"Yeah. Good luck, Lord," Lil' Rico said, shoving the money into his skinny jeans.

"I'll hit you soon," Malik said, hopping in his car to pull off.

West Virginia

56

Boss was on the road driving in a Chevy Malibu Rental on the highway to see his father in Bruceton Mills, West VA at a maximum-security federal prison called Hazelton USP. After speaking to his mother, she convinced him to go pay him a visit because at the end of the day he was still his father. Boss didn't have nothing against his father at all. The two would write and talk daily but Boss was so focused on chasing money, his dad wasn't a real priority at the moment.

His pops was a big part of his life even though he was locked up most of his life, Boss knew how it was to be lockdown so he was understanding. Since his first lick a couple of weeks ago he had been saving money, he'd just sold the pounds of weed to his homies because he wasn't planning on selling weed anymore. He gave two keys to Animal and Malik.

Now he was waiting on his uncle to give him the details of his new lick because he was hungry, and he had no remorse in killing. Boss pulled up the long entrance to see two other prisons as he rode up the hill that went a mile until he saw the large wall with prison guards in a booth with shotguns.

"How can we help you boy," one of the racist COs said, spitting out chewing tobacco.

Boss wanted to check him out. This wasn't his first visit here and he knew how hard the guards made it on inmates' families to prevent them from coming back to visit their loved ones.

"I'm here to visit my father," Boss said, giving the C.O. his I.D. and license. Once he was let inside, he parked in a visitor's spot and walked inside ready to go through another process.

Ty Stone was in his unit in the law library doing some studying on a couple of new cases that had just won appeals in the Supreme Court. He heard his name called from the office, he looked back, and one of the two officers yelled that he had a visit which was surprising.

"Okay, big homie. You about to go dance with your star son, have a good one," his neighbor said. He was a blond kid from New York with a life sentence plus one-hundred and twenty years.

"Good lookin', Joe," Ty Stone said as he went upstairs to his cell to put on some fresh clothes, Muslim oil and to brush his teeth, luckily he recently got a hair-cut so he looked clean.

Twenty minutes later he walked into the visitor's room to see other inmates with their family and loved ones. When he looked around, he saw Boss sitting there with long dreads looking like a real Chi-Raq nigga.

"Son, what's up," Ty Stone said, hugging his son.

"Good to see you. You're looking good, old man."

"I'm just trying to stay alive. What brings you out? I haven't seen you in three years," Ty said.

"I just wanted to show some love."

"A'ight, I spoke to your mother the other night she says you're doing good. You still working?"

"Not really pops, you know how it is. I'm just trying to make a living."

"I understand but be careful, nowadays niggas are wolves in lamb clothing. There are many different kinds of people in the world and you can never assume that everyone will react to your strategies. Choose your victims and opponents carefully. When you meet a sword, draw your sword. Do not recite poetry to one who is not a poet," his father said who was a man of wise words.

"I'm focused, pops. My eyes are open."

"Good, I never want to see you in the field but you're a man now and men make choices, but we have to stand on our choices son. Too many so-called gangstas snitching, the game is dangerous."

"I see it everyday niggas get knocked with the motherload and come home talking about they let them go with a warning," Boss said making his pops laugh. "That makes good sense, but I visited Iman Sa'id last week and he is sharp. He sends his love."

"Thank you, he's a good man. He taught me a lot. He wrote me from time to time back in the day. He had over forty bodies under his belt. All the gangstas like Jeff Fort, Jermaine Freeman, and James Cogswell all looked up to him."

"That's crazy, I ain't know that his son was a problem, too, but he vanished,'" Ty said confusingly because Iman Sa'id's son Evil Stone had the city scared to come outside, and the two were close before he disappeared.

"How's your appeal looking?"

"Trust in Allah's hands. I have left it to the man above but I'm doing my part."

Romell Tukes

Chapter 10

Cook County Jail

Fame just stepped outside of the jail gates in a fresh New Balmain outfit and saw his little brother parked in the lot. Fame had to come straight to the county jail for ten days for a bench warrant after doing all his time but he was glad to finally be home.

The news he'd received last month of his best friend Loso being killed crushed him deeply, both of them had a lot of rank in their BD gang. At thirty-years-old Fame missed a lot of time out of his life due to being stuck in prison. He was from Buff City and now with Loso cut out of the picture he was up, and he had plans to change a lot of shit. First, he was hell-bent on finding Loso's killer. Somebody wanted them dead and if they ran up in his crib and killed his mother, Fame knew it had to be a robbery. He knew Loso was hood rich.

Fame was a tall, skinny, ugly, bucktooth nigga with a high top fade but his confidence was so high he would make a bitch jump out there.

"L's up, nigga," his little brother Mula said hopping out of the truck in a Gucci outfit with a big face Rolex and bear-hugging his older brother.

Mula was from O-Block but he now lived on the Westside in L Town, he was also BD in a hood full of New Breeds and 4s. He was getting money with Face Stone, one of the biggest drug dealers in the city.

"You look solid, Joe," Fame said, checking out little bro's watch.

"Nigga, I got you one too," Mula said pulling out a Rolex box.

Fame rushed to open it, it was a Sky-Dweller with diamonds in the face. "That's love gratitude, bro."

"You ain't seen nothing just wait until you see the Chevrolet Camaro it's blue with black stripes, I got you."

"You ain't gotta do that for me."

"On gang, bro, it's a new era," Mula said as they climbed in the Range pulling off.

Mula updated his brother about everything going on in the city but Fame already knew about most of the events because in Cook County Jail niggas talked about everybody's dealings. Mula also had two bitches waiting for Fame at his condo ready to fuck and suck all those years out of him he suffered.

Southside, Chi-Town

Boss entered Uncle Jay's dirty apartment to see that he had on the same dirty robe he had on weeks ago. The apartment had rodents everywhere, dirty dishes, and dirty clothes. Boss had only been there twice, and he didn't want to come back.

"Nephew, it's good to see you," Uncle Jay said, moving all types of shit from his couch so Boss could sit.

"I'm standing. What's up, Joe, what you got for me?" Boss said trying not to stick around long because he was already starting to itch.

"His name is Sin G. He lives on the outskirts in Chicago Heights. He moves heavy dope and he's a Spanish cat that's real low key and smart."

"He banging?"

"Nah, he just about getting money but he supplies the Satan Disciples and the Maniacs on the Westside. His younger brother is one of the head Dollar Bill niggas."

"How you know all this shit when you never leave the house?" Boss asked as he laughed.

"I got eyes and hoes everywhere youngin' I used to be somebody out here."

"You got his location? I need everything to be accurate."

"I'm two steps ahead of you, remember. He lives on Main Street where your GD guys at."

"Damn," Boss said. "Everybody knows I'm over there and my gang shares that hood with the LKs."

"He lives in the cut. in a smoke gray, brick apartment building on the second floor. This his lowkey spot nephew, he got a house with his wife and kids in Robins, IL but I'm sure nothing is in there, he's too smart for that."

"Okay, text me the addy and when it's done, I'll be back," Boss said walking at with a new mission on his mind

Chicago Heights, IL

Chicago Heights was the outskirts of the city but it was just as dangerous. Niggas were dying left and right from gang violence. This was Sin G's home and where he sold his keys of dope, there were only a couple of more big-time hustlers in the area, but he was number one. Sin G was Puerto Rican, in his mid-twenties, and a smart hustler. He was never into gang banging, he left that to his brother Cash Bay who was a wild boy in the streets.

Sin G was sitting in his apartment at his dining room table filled with a stack of money laced in rubber bands. The money machine was counting the money he picked up earlier from his workers. Every Monday night Sin G would do this alone because he didn't trust a soul, not even his own mother or brother.

This was his second stash house. The other house is where he kept his drugs and that was in the Westside of Chicago. He kept his money here after pickups for a day or two until he invested it in bank accounts and two of his businesses he owned. He hated the loud noise of the money machine, but he had no other choice. He didn't have time to sit and count hundreds to thousands of dollars.

Sin G just so happened to look at the front door and saw that the bottom and top lock was unlocked. He knew he was slipping as he got up to lock it. When he got within two feet of the door, *Boom!* His door was kicked open with ease as three, masked men dressed in all black rushed in with guns drawn.

"Get down, nigga!" Animal yelled, forcing Sin G on his face on the oak wood floor.

Malik and Boss saw money all over the table in neat stacks in rubber bands as a money machine was still counting the money.

They tossed all the money in the garbage bags, even the money in the machine as Animal held his foot on Sin G's head.

"Where's the rest?" Boss asked after filling two bags of money.

"In my mattress in my bedroom, then I swear I have nothing else," Sin G cried with his face on the floor watching Malik ramshacked his kitchen while Boss was in the back room. Sin G was never robbed, he tried to peace this shit up in his head, but he kept coming up short.

Minutes later Boss came from the back with a Louis Vuttion duffle bag full of money and a big smile.

"We can leave now," Boss said as Malik grabbed the two bags.

"Who sent you? Let me guess, Ole Jay? That nigga—"

Bloc! Bloc! Bloc! Bloc!

Animal shot him in the back of his head before he could even finish his sentence.

"Damn, Joe you should have let him finish," Boss said as they exit, Animal just shrugged his shoulders.

Two Days Later

Boss popped up at Uncle Jay with a Jamspat backpack in his hand, before he could even knock the door flew open. His uncle stood there with big eyes. Boss walked in to see the red-haired hooker sitting on the couch in a dress and heels as if she was about to go trick.

"It's ten o'clock at night bitch be back before I am. And if you ain't got over a stack don't bring that ass back," Uncle Jay said in his pimp voice.

She eyed Boss' Gucci attire wishing she could be his hoe. She stood up and her little ass jiggled, then she bent over showing her bare pussy lips.

"You got your hands full," Boss said as she closed the door.

"This pimp game is all I know," he said but without her, he would be dope sick every day.

"I hear you, Joe. Here is your cut from that lick," Boss said, tossing him the backpack.

He opened it like a kid opening presents on Christmas morning. When Uncle Jay saw the money, he wanted to cry and scream because this was the most money he'd seen in over a decade. Back in the day he would be pimping five or six hoes in one night and be living like a king before he became an addict.

"Wow, how much is this? It's too much to count," he said seriously.

Boss laughed. "Forty thousand, nigga. You hit the lick right on the target."

"I know what I know youngin' trust me."

"You know him or something?"

"Nah, not really just used to watch him. Why?"

"No reason," Boss said knowing there was more to the story but as long as he was paid shit was voided.

"Did he have any drugs, keys, or bricks?"

"Nana we looked."

"Ooohhh."

"You're still getting high off tha dope, Unc?"

"Hell no, don't disrespect me like that. I just got some clients looking for weight!" he yelled.

"A'ight hit me when you ready again." Boss walked out knowing his uncle was lying because he saw a line of dope on the mirror under the living room table.

The crew divided the 240,500 into three then they all bust down 8% of the profit for Jay, but the crew was all happy and with their luck, they were not looking back now.

Romell Tukes

Chapter 11

Buff City

Lil' BD and Hitler were in a trap house in the basement with a thick, chunky chick from Capitol Hill where Hitler was from but he got around.

"Ugh, shittt," Tiff moaned, she was on all fours as Hitler fucked her from behind while she sucked Lil' BD's dick like a wild animal.

Hitler long stroke and pounded her big pussy out while smacking her ass making her big ass wobble.

"Suck that shit, eat that dick, bitch," Lil' BD moaned as she gulped his dick and slurped his pre-cum like noodles.

Tiff was a head doctor, she loved sucking good dick. She took him in the back of her throat as Hitler rammed her body back and forth, he was seconds from cumming and she picked up the pace.

"Ohhhh, fuckkk! Uggg—" Tiff cried out as Hitler's big, fat, curved dick stretched her pussy walls apart.

Lil' BD nutted as she forced her head down to his pubic hairs so she could shove every inch down her throat.

"Mmmhhhmmm," she moaned, sucking Lil' BD's mandingo dry as semen spilled out of her mouth. She sucked until he went limp.

Hitler felt Tiff's warm cum coating his dick as he pulled out and busted a thick load of his seeds on her ass.

"My turn." Tiff laid on her back lifting her legs all the way back so one could enter her ass hole and the other could enter her pussy. She loved to be gangbanged especially in her ass that turned her on.

Hitler and Lil' BD were getting dressed as they looked at each other and knew there was no way their dicks were going to be that close and her pussy was stanky they couldn't take the smell no more.

"We gotta go handle some business with Hops across town but maybe next time," Hitler said fully dressed in a Palm Angel grey sweatsuit, now pulling his dreads into a ponytail.

"Oh, it's like that? After I been down here two hours sucking and fucking y'all niggas!" she yelled getting dressed, she was pissed. Then they heard gunshots ring out from down the block which was all day.

"It's ten p.m., I gotta go home anyway. Y'all niggas ain't shit. You gonna at least pay for my uber."

"Shit we ain't Uber you over here, bitch," Lil' BD said.

She rolled her big eyes at him. Hitler led her upstairs to escort her out the front door. Lil BD went out back with the gang who was in the back yard with pipes everywhere. They had ADs, SKs, Mac-10s, and a ton of Dracos for wartime.

"What was the shots?" Lil' BD asked as he walked up to the nine niggas smoking and looking for trouble like most youngins in the city.

"SB and Mikey G just shot at some Vice Lords. Them niggas know they not allowed over here. They got beef with them three-hundred and O-Block niggas so we one-hundred block it's OTF, Joe," Louis said.

"That's void, me and Hitler about to slide to his hood on seventy-first."

"You got your pole?"

"Always," Lil BD said, pulling out a Glock 17 with an extended clip and 30 rounds.

Hitler walked onto the block to see it was pitch black as always, he was a Four Corner Hustler as most called a 7. Everybody respected him because his older brother started the gang before the police killed him in broad daylight outside of his home.

Hitler was the same age as Lil' BD, he was a vicious robber. It was more of a hobby than anything. His grandmother raised him, and his real name was Blake, but the streets named him after his brother, Hitler. He was short at five-nine compared to Lil' BD. He was a pretty boy, red nigga with long dreads and nice charm that got the ladies. He and Lil' BD have been best friends forever; they were like brothers if not deeper.

"We out, fam," Hitler told everybody as he and Lil' BD made their way to Hitler's old Honda Civic, to head across town to hit a lick. Lately, the two had been robbing gas stations and tourists downtown.

Boss just arrived in his Uncle's crib to see that he had on a fresh suit with shoes as if he was about to step out to play ball.

"I see niggas start getting money and start looking like Penny," Boss said seeing that the crib was still dirty.

"Money has its own appearance young blood a little money can make a broke nigga look like a million dollars."

"Facts, but what's up? You hit me up when I was in the middle of some pussy," Boss said being honest because he was smashing his wife before his Uncle blew his phone up.

"Pussy is a good man's downfall, champ. I have seen a lot of good pussy swallow niggas whole so think outside tha pussy box. Why you think I be pimpin' bitches? I'm heartless but that's the way you have to be or these hoes will walk all over it."

"True that's why I don't fuck with hoes. Now, what's going on?" Boss asked.

"Our next nigga is Big Scoop. He's a New bread nigga from the Westside in a hood called the Village. This nigga is bigger than Big Pun, Heavy D, and Biggie all together. He's hood rich I sent one of my hoes at him a while back and now it's time."

"Them new Bread niggas roll deep, and they be getting a little of money," Boss added.

"A little, shit that's an understatement, nephew. But he travels with a crew, so you need to have some solid niggas on this one."

"A'ight send me his location later," Boss said ready to leave.

"That's the only issue. I don't have no location on him, all I know is every night he goes to McDonald's drive-thru before midnight in the Village."

"A'ight, I'll figure it out, Joe. You need to get one of your hoes to clean this please."

"My hoes work for a fee, not for free," Uncle Jay said as Boss made his way out as his woman walked inside with a black eye that he'd given her earlier.

The Next Night

Downtown, Chi-town

Club Dream was a new club across the street from Club Secrets and tonight it was lit with women, ballers, and young niggas but everybody came out to enjoy themselves. Boss and his crew were in the lower level of the dark club in a private booth area popping bottles of Henny and Ciroc, regular hood nigga shit in the club.

"Nigga, ain't you on parole? How you be out all night?"

"My P.O. didn't give me a curfew, she trying to fuck a nigga for real. Why, nigga?" Animal asked Malik.

"Just asking, Joe," Malik stated.

"When will you all be ready again? Because we got another lick but this area a nigga gotta drill some shit you dig," Boss said drinking coconut Ciroc like water.

"I'm ready now," Animal said and Malik nodded.

"It's a nigga named, Big Scoop from the village."

"Oh, yeah, the new bread nigga?" Animal said.

"Yeah. You know him?" Boss asked, hoping he did so they could have an easy layout.

"Nah, but I heard he be looking out for all them niggas. I heard he got a big boy," Animal said.

"I've got a plan, but I'm hearing he rolls with a crew. So, I don't know if we need more people?" Boss said but was assigned at the same time.

"My little cousin, Rico is a standup young nigga. I think we should bring him in as the driver or something or for back up. What y'all think?" Malik asked.

"I don't care as long as he don't get none of my cut," Animal stated seriously.

"Nigga, we all gave to your special helper," Malik added

"Oh, yeah, I forgot about that."

"As long as we can trust him then bring him but only on one mission. We don't know what's installed for us, Joe," Boss said.

"No question. Now let's toast and hit this dance floor," Malik said as they all cheered and made their way to the dance floor.

All three men were dripping in designer clothes. When the females asked who they were, they told them Chi'Raq Gangstas.

Chapter 12

The Village, West Chi'Raq

Big Scoop drove down East Street in his big boy, all black Cadillac Escalade truck sitting on 28-inch rims. He had a few behind him as always in a BMW truck making his way to McDonald's as he did every night at 11:15 p.m. for years. He weighed well over 300 pounds. He was big, black, ugly, and hood rich. Big Scoop was a high-ranking member of the New bread only because he took care of his guys in the streets and prison.

Niggas was willing to die for him especially his little homie, Shaw who was across town trapping as always. Shaw was his youngin' and he handled all of Big Scoop's business affairs.

After being in the game for twenty years Big Scoop was never arrested, he hustled smart and grinded smarter. He cleaned this money and opened two bail bondsman shops on the Westside. He was born and raised on the Westside of Chi-rag in L town and The Village where it was all crabs in a bucket.

Big Scoop pulled into Mcdonald's drive-thru to see another SUV in front of him and the cars were behind the Tahoe. Big Scoop bobbed his head to the new Twista song one of his favorite rappers and a close friend who went to school with him. He saw a van behind him, and his guys were behind the van waiting in line. Once he was up to order his food at the intercom he turned down his loud music that shook the block.

"I will like a number two, with extra mayo, a number four, and a number six."

"Sir, sir, sir please we go through this every night. You have to speak into the intercom," a young lady said, taking his order.

"Bitch!"

"Excuse me,"

"I said a number six—two—four—and seven with extra mayoooo—" he said, dragging out his words.

"Thank you, you can pull up," she said. I hate this stanking nigga," the cashier said unaware her mic was still on.

Big Scoop laughed because he was going to pay one of his homegirls to come stomp her out.

"I think it's time," Boss told Animal as they were behind the BMW truck and Malik and Rico were in a van behind Big Scoop and in front of his guys.

Boss saw there were four niggas in the BMW blasting loud music, he screwed a silencer onto his pistol and pulled his face mask down. Animal was driving.

"Stick to the plan, Joe," Boss said as he hopped out.

Like clockwork, Malik hopped out of the passenger side of the van. Big Scoop's goons watched Malik as they all had their windows down.

"Nigga, you going to order?" the driver asked Malik unaware of the killer lurking.

Psst! Psst! Psst! Psst! Psst! Psst! Psst! Psst!

Boss killed all four men in the BMW truck holding him at gunpoint as he waited at the window for his food. Boss was behind him and Malik was on his side with his gun on his lap aimed at him, shaking like a rookie cop on the first day on the job.

"Pull off slowly," Boss said.

"Can I at least get my food—"

Whack!

Boss slapped him in the head with his gun.

"Okay—" Big Scoop pulled off. Rico and Animal followed the truck until they got away from the crime scene they'd just left.

"Where the money and drugs?" Boss asked driving through the main streets as nobody was out except a couple of dope fiends running in and out of traps.

"It's on Broadway, my man is there. I can get you whatever you need, please spare me I got ten kilos."

"Nigga, shut up and call him. Tell him to bring everything you have to Congress Park alone in twenty minutes or you a goner." Boss handed him a burnout phone as he stopped. He told Shaw who was asking is he sure and he told him yeah they had no choice.

"Call the guys," Boss said.

Malik was already on the phone with them confirming they'd got the load. "Job well done," Malik said.

"Good. Where y'all want me to drop y'all off?" Big Scoop said as both men laughed before filling his body up with hot bullets.

When they were done Big Scoop had fifty-eight holes in him and his head looked like swiss cheese. Rico and Animal pulled up minutes later while they were standing in the school entrance driveway.

Southside

Kimmie called Jenny over to her job at a strip club called Red Diamond, Jenny wasn't much of a club person. She'd been laying low lately because summertime in the Southside was like World War IV. Jenny was outside in her car watching thirsty niggas rush in the club to trick off their money like true clowns. She saw Kimmie walk out of the club in heels and a tight dress with ass and titties hanging as niggas grabbed her arms trying to holler. Kimmie wasn't in the mode for none of that shit, she saw Jenny's car and made her way over to her.

"What's up, girl? You look vexed," Jenny said, seeing bags under her eyes and a stressful look.

"Imagining so much," she said as she just started to cry like a baby. Jenny was numb to emotions, so she didn't really know what to say or do.

"What's wrong?"

"You remember, Loso?"

"Of course," Jenny said, wondering if she knew she had anything to do with his death.

"This nigga gave me HIV. I wasn't feeling good the other day and I went to the clinic. These people tell me I got the monster and I know it was him, he's the only nigga who fucked me raw. Plus, I wasn't fucking like that," she said wiping her tears not knowing what to say.

"Damn, Kimmie, I'm keeping you in my prayers."

"Prayers!" Kimmie yelled looking at her crazy before she rushed out of her car back into the club a hot mess.

"Bitch, I'm not the one with HIV!" Jenny yelled out her window as a couple of the niggas heading inside the club heard the commotion.

Animal was in a designer outlet doing some shopping. The big Scoop lick was big-time they all received 140K apiece after taking Rico and Uncle Jay's cut.

Big Scoop also had fifteen keys of coke each person got five keys apiece they all put away for a rainy day.

Animal planned to buy a car today he'd just bought an Audemar Piguet watch earlier from a famous jewelry store downtown.

He walked into the Louis Vuttion store and started going crazy on belts, shoes, outfits, scarves, sweaters, and underclothes. As he was shopping, he saw the baddest Spanish bitch he'd ever seen in white tights and heels with crazy ass and curves with no stomach.

Animal tried not to stare but he wasn't the only one staring at women who looked like an upscale Eva Longoria. She was coming his way to look at some heels when he saw that she had clear, grey eyes and felt his dick jump.

"It's rude to stare," she said in a sweet calm voice.

"I'm sorry I just never saw a woman as beautiful as you," he said as she eyed his big muscles and smiled. "Good line. Maybe a younger woman would fall for it," she quipped.

"I don't know, ma. I can only say how I feel but I'll give the world to have someone like you."

"I think you may be barking up the wrong tree."

"If I am it's worth the risk," he said looking into her eyes trying not to get lost.

"You're handsome and chasing a bag I see. But what can you offer a woman like me? I'm not your everyday type and I have my own," she said as niggas walked past trying to eavesdrop.

"I can only offer you love and all of me, the best of me," he said as she smiled and walked off. "Damn—" he said, cursing himself watching her hips and ass sway as he wondered what her culture was.

After forty minutes of shopping, he was ready to cash out, all his items came up to 32K which he paid in cash.

"Oh, the Spanish lady in the Padres left this for you. She is a regular, I think she's super-rich or some shit," the fat black cashier chick said as she handed him a piece of paper.

Animal read the paper that said, *I like your energy and vibes. Call me.* A phone number was nearly scrawled below the words.

He was so happy he almost forgot the LV bags before leaving.

Romell Tukes

Chapter 13

Downtown, Chicago

Boss and Rosie got out of Uber at the luxury car dealership.

"Where is your car?" Rosie asked as the summer heat beamed on her forehead, she covered her forehead with her hands.

"Chill, come on," Boss said, walking inside the lot until he saw a salesman walking around, checking on the new shipments of cars they'd received last night.

"Excuse me, I'm Tyrell, I called a couple of days ago for my orders."

"Okay, Mr. Johnson. Yes, your shipment is in the back lot, sir. We've been waiting on you since we received your payment," the young black man said in a suit leading them to the back as they passed BMWs, Rolls Royces, Porsches, and McLarens.

"Tyrell, what the hell is he talking about?" asked Rosie, confused and unaware of his recent dealings because he kept his private life separate from his personal life.

"I am getting one day," Boss said, pointing at a new White Wraith spinning on a showcase rack.

Rosie laughed at him while holding his hand. "Maybe I should start selling weed too," she whispered, and he laughed.

"Here you guys go," the salesman said pointing at a red Audi R8, a red Maserati Grant Cape, SP.

"Oh shit, baby," Rosie stated speechless looking at the red Maserati.

"Here go the keys, all the paperwork was already handled by my boss so enjoy." The salesman passed Boss both sets of keys.

"Thank you. Here you go, baby." Boss tossed Rosie the keys to the Maserati as he made his way over to the Audi admiring the black leather seats and new car smell.

"Babe, how could you afford these?" she asked, sitting inside the peanut butter seats of her Maserati.

Boss sold all the drugs from all his prior licks and had enough money to treat himself and her while putting some to the side for a rainy day.

"Let's go shopping before the Fendi and Gucci store close," he said.

She was so happy she wanted to cry. "I'm fucking you all night and I am doing that thing you like me to do," she said starting up the quiet engine for her luxury car as he smiled.

They raced off on the way to do some shopping. Boss knew she deserved every bit of being spoiled because she was with him in hard times and good times.

Boss was in his mom's house watching TV while she was at work. He would come through from time to time to check on Lil' BD. Lil' BD hadn't been home in four days, but he came to get some sleep in peace. He had to meet Hitler and Main Street because he said he had something to holler at him about.

"Bro, what's up?" Lil' BD said coming out of his room unaware he was there because he rarely came around.

"Ain't shit family. How you doing, Joe?" Boss said, looking at his brother's old Jordan sneakers.

Last month Boss tried to give his mom and little bro some money, but they refused it. He knew his mom would but he didn't expect his bro to be on that.

"I'm about to head across town."

"Before you go take this." Boss puled out 5K.

"Nah, bro, I'm good."

"My money ain't no good, BD?"

"It's not that, bro. I rather get it out the mud. I don't take handouts, I am BD bro, we get it out the struggle," Lil' BD said firmly.

"I'm not your ops or none of them goofy niggas in the streets. I'm your blood, your brother, just remember that Joe," Boss said, feeling a little offended by his comment.

"Facts, I'll see you later," Lil' BD said slamming the door behind him as Boss looked at all the photos of black activists all over his living room.

The apartment he grew up in was decked out with Versace couches, love seats, replica antique, ceiling fans, a beautiful view of the city from the terrace, wall to wall rugs, a state of the art surround sound system, four bedrooms, two private walk-in bathrooms, and a wood panel library with black civil rights fighters.

Boss sat there dumbfounded feeling as if his little brother was changing right before his eyes, but he felt there was more to what he was seeing but he couldn't put his finger on it.

Stoney Island

Hitler and Lil' BD were in the Stoney Island area on the southside, parked across the street from a gas station in an apartment complex parking lot.

"That's him right there," Hitler said pointing at the African man pumping people's gas and collecting the money, placing it in his pants pockets.

"It's almost eleven at night and niggas still getting gas?" Lil' BD said.

"Nigga it's a twenty-four-hour gas station."

"I see that goofy nigga," Lil' BD said thinking about how his brother tried to play him earlier as if he couldn't hold his own.

"Come on let's slide it's empty," Hitler said, pulling his face mask down as Lil BD followed his lead.

Muhammad had just started working as a gas station attendant two days ago to support his family who'd just arrived in the states weeks ago from a small town called Da Aar in South Africa. Today was a business day. It was Friday, but he didn't expect to make four-hundred dollars in tips and twenty-seven hundred in gas total gross.

He went inside the gas station to take a piss, he saw no other cars were coming so he took a break. When Muhammad walked back out front he was singing his favorite motherland song by *Enoch Santonya* until he saw the two men with big guns pointed at him.

"Me don't want no problem," Muhammad said scared to death.

"Give me the money," Hitler said as they watched him closely go in his pockets to pull out a wad of money.

Lil' BD went to snatch the money out of his hand, once he got the money, he looked at Hitler and they turned to leave as they planned.

Out of the corner of Lil' BD's eyes, he saw Muhammad reaching for something which made him turn on his heels and fire two shots into Muhammad's chest.

Muhammad's old .22 Revolver fell onto the floor and his body collapsed in a puddle of gas from a large gas container. Muhammad's boss gave him a gun to use in situations like this, to defend himself because Chicago was a deadly area at night especially. Both men saw that Muhammad was dead and they ran to the Honda, then raced off, watching customers pull into the gas station in their rearview.

103 Luella Precinct

Lil' Rico was locked up in the police station's integration room for a gun charge he caught this morning driving around in his new Cadillac CTS-V he'd coped with the money he received from the Big Scoop's lick. Lil' Rico had never gone to jail and he was sweating bullets. A Spanish cop walked into the room, seeing that Rico looked like he was about to cry.

"Loosen up, it could be worse. I'm officer, D.T. Rodriguez. I'm giving you a lawyer call, but you know your rights, correct?"

"Yes, sir, but what if I give you some information? Could I avoid jail time?" Rico said getting straight to the point.

Rodriguez cleared his throat and sat up straight. Normally he had to force a sweet talk by a criminal to snitch but that was too sweet for him.

"Maybe. What do you have for me?"

"A couple of weeks ago a four men crew was murdered in a McDonald's drive-thru and that same night Big Scoop was killed in his truck behind a school. I know who did it."

Rodriquez's eyes widened because those cases popped up on his desk weeks ago, but he had no lead until now. He had been watching Big Scoop and his new Bread gang for years but the man was too smart.

"How do you know this?" Rodriquez asked.

"I was there with them."

"With who?"

"The Chi'Raq Gangsta crew. My cousin Malik is down with them and I was driving watching their back."

"Okay, let's start from the top," Rodriguez said, pulling out a pen and pad knowing he was on to something.

Romell Tukes

Chapter 14

Downtown, Chi-Town

Malik and Simone were both dressed to impress so they went out for dinner at a nice, classy restaurant. Malik was stacking money, besides the mustang he coped and a couple of bands he was spending on his girl. Life was perfect but lately, he was feeling a come up he was overwhelmed into cashing a bag.

"Baby this place is nice I never knew this spot was over here and I work down the block," Simone said looking around the dining room with candlelight tables, thick rugs, fancy wall paintings, and fancy food neither one of them could pronounce.

"Yeah, I looked it up," he replied looking at her titties sitting up perfectly in her Chanel strap dress.

"You spent a lot of money on Michigan Ave at the mall, baby. Where are you getting that type of money from?" she said in a low pitch tone, while he cut his well-done steak

"Just know we are going to be good. I don't even want you to work no more, Simone. You bust your ass at that store, you deserve a better lifestyle."

"I'm not going to get in trouble, babe. I do need a favor?" he asked.

"Anything, love."

"I need you to plug me in with your cousin, Face," he said as she gave him a look like she knew what he was into because Face was the biggest dope connect in the city.

"I'll speak to him, but you know he don't fuck with too many people niggas. Since they be turning and ratting on everybody," Simone said knowing how her cousin who she loved.

"Okay, thanks but let's take this show home and smoke while you feed me dessert."

"I would love to, big daddy," she said blushing as they left the restaurant.

A small plan was about to be in full motion he just needed to holler at them guys.

Uncle Jay found a new crib on Clyde Street in the cut near a post office and hair salon. This area was a big moneymaker for pimps. He even found a new, young, cute, white bitch thanks to Red, his main bitch.

"Daddy can we go get something to eat?'" Cardine asked, flashing her blue eyes, and showing off her petite frame in shorts.

"Yeah. But come back because I got three Johns coming over to see you," he said to Cardine as Red walked out the back room.

'How about me, any dates, daddy?" Red asked.

"No bitch, but one of your Johns coming so see her in the next hour. So, y'all go ahead and come back," Uncle Jay said looking at Cardine's sexy walk.

He was fucking her for days breaking her in, she was twenty-three-years old and her pussy was tight and good. Plus, her head game was good but not better than Red's. Once they left, he text Boss asking him what apartment since he was outside. Jay had a new mission for his nephew, he took his time with this one.

Boss saw Uncle Jay's door open as he said it would be, Boss walked inside the clean new apartment and saw the new flat screen, rugs, furniture, and tables, he was shocked.

"Damn, Uncle, you clean up well."

"Thank you, nephew. Have a seat," Uncle Jay said smiling.

"A'ight I saw a cute blonde headed downstairs."

"Yeah, that's fresh meat in my cattle youngin and her pussy tight."

"I believe you."

"You want a test drive, nephew? I don't know if you can handle that, she a wild one."

"Nah, I'm good."

"A'ight, but I got a new mission. She should be easy but it's her brother who you have to worry about."

"Who is she?"

"A Vice Lord chick named Shayla from the Westside. She's in Holy City, she's the Godmother for the CVL's. So, whatever you do be smart them niggas play for keeps."

"I already know but where he lives."

84

"She got four spots out there, but I can't pinpoint. She is out of town now but she is major, kid," Uncle Jay said seriously.

"I've heard of her, let me get the crew together. I'll be in touch soon."

"That's what I like to hear but what do you call yourself? Every crew got a name that's how the stones got started," Jay said as his two hoes walked in with Chinese food.

"Chi'Raq Gangstas," Boss said walking out.

University of Chicago

Jenny was pulled out of her school parking area after a long day of school and exams. It was a rainy, humid day in the city so she planned to go over to her boyfriend's house and feed his dog sonic. He was overseas playing basketball, but he was supposed to be back in a week or so.

Her boyfriend Larry was cool and he wasn't a street nigga but they had a good, strong connection. Every nigga wanted Jenny, but she didn't give niggas time of the day because she was the relation-ship type.

She drove to Larry's condo blocks away from her college to feed his dogs then she planned to go home to get some rest. The next week she was moving into her new crib to get away from her hood because just last night alone six bodies dropped. Minutes later, she was walking into Larry condo build which was nice with a view of the Chicago River and tall skyrise buildings.

Once in the condo, she saw it was a little dirty, so she wasted no time cleaning up the place which was large upstairs and down-stairs. A dual staircase, a living room connected to a dining room and bath, Brazilian Oak hardwood floors, high ceilings, heated floors, the master bedrooms, and two private master bathrooms, and his/her walk-in closets.

As Jenny was picking up clothing in the living room, she heard a noise upstairs, she went upstairs to check on the red nose pitbull they called buddy. To her surprise, the pit was sleeping in the first room on the floor.

85

Jenny continued to hear noise and banging as she walked down the hallway, when stopped outside of Larry's bedroom she heard the noise loud and clear as she slowly opened the door.

"Ugggghhhh! Yyyeeessss—fuckkk meee!" a woman moaned, riding his dick like a Western cowgirl.

Jenny saw a big black ass bouncing up and down on her man's dick and the smell of sex filled the air. The hard rain outside banged on the glass window as thunder struck outside and she watched the woman pop her ass on his big dick as they both moaned.

"I love you, boo," Larry said as her pussy gripped his dick making him cum.

"Excuse me—" Jenny finally said.

They both jumped up but when Jenny saw who the bitch was she wanted to whip her ass.

"Baby, how you get in—" he said, forgetting he had given her a key. "What are you doing here? This isn't what it looks like," he said getting dressed as cum was leaked from his dick.

"Kimmie, how could you?" Jenny said, looking at the same bitch she brought around her man many times and never would've pictured this.

"Jenny, I'm sorry he paid me fifty-five hundred dollars."

"Shut up!" Larry yelled, walking towards Jenny.

"Nigga, don't come near me you dirty nigga. You're dead to me both of you," she said. Kimmie started to cry. "Did you at least tell him you were HIV positive?" Jenny said.

Kimmie shook her head no.

"What! Bitch you got HIV?" he yelled.

"Yes, I'm sorry," she said standing in the corner naked, showing her thick, sexy, dancer body with his cum dripping down her legs.

"Hope you two are happy together." Jenny headed for the door, hearing them yell back and forth. As he was yelling how could she let him fuck her raw?

Jenny was glad she hadn't fuck him in months because she wouldn't know what she would do if she caught something but she wondered how long they'd been fucking.

Jenny was on her way to the nearest clinic to get checked for everything because she didn't know how long their affair was going on for. They always used condoms because she didn't trust him when he was an overseas playing ball. She knew he was fucking women in other counties, so she just wanted to be safe.

Romell Tukes

Chapter 15

Holy City, West Chi-Town

Shayla was in one of her apartments in her hood on the Westside in the violent area known as Holy City. She stroked her side nigga's dick from the base to the tip while sucking on his balls as he laid in her king-size bed with the curtains covering all angles of the bed. She coated his big, brown, perfect dick with saliva as she moaned and licked around the tip before she started sucking the head like a piece of now or later candy.

"Hmmmmm," he moaned as she took him down her warm throat, she bopped her head up and down causing her wig to almost come off. The loud noise of sucking and slurping could be heard outside as his dick rammed in and out her swallow cheeks.

"Shit, I'm cumming," he cried with his face and neck tightened as if he was stuck.

Shayla used her thick lips to massage his dick as she picked up the pace, she felt his cum enter her mouth. She sucked out his salty cum then spit it back out on his dick and did tongue tricks on his tip, then he popped his dick out of her mouth and lifted her up so they could fuck.

"Don't get used to that great moment. Now fuck me good and make me cum," she said bending over showing him her round wide ass with flowers tattooed on her ass cheeks.

Her pussy was bald and small with a long slit pairing her dark pussy lips and her large clit pumped out. Shayla's side nigga, Larry licked her dripping pussy and spread her big ass cheeks apart, then entered her throbbing tight, wet pussy walls.

"Ugggghhh fuck nigga-a-a!" Shayla yelled as his big, fat, long dick stretched her walls and he thrust in her going deeper with long, slow strokes. She grabbed her pillow trying to throw her ass back as he banged her harder. "Ahhhh, I-I can't take it don't stop—" she moaned in pleasure as she tightened her pussy on his dick looking at him while catching a big orgasm.

"Oooohhh, baby!" she yelled as he violently drove his pelvis deep into her ass about to nut.

"Aaahhhh sssss, yesss, Larry! I'm cumminggg!" she screamed, sweating as her body flew back and forth and her wig flew on the floor showing her four, thick, short nappy braids which made Larry close his eyes because looking at her was now fucking up his nut.

Psst! Larry's tall body leaned forward falling on Shayla's back. She was so caught up in her screams and pleasure she didn't even see or hear what was going on.

"Nigga what the fuck you doing, Larry?" she said feeling his body collapse on hers.

When she saw he wasn't moving and blood leaking on her back she pushed him off her. "Oh, my God!" she yelled seeing that he was dead, and three guns were pointed at him.

Shayla covered her body which was shaped like a Coca-Cola bottle, she was in her twenties, but she had the body of a goddess and it was all hers. She was a cute chick, but she only fucked with ballers. Larry was an overseas basketball player. She knew he had a bitch named Jenny, but he was only a play toy.

Her brother was the real plug, but he was normally down South while he let her control the Chicago drug trade then she had ten more brothers locked up.

"You know what this is," Malik said as Shayla looked at him oddly.

"Malik!" she yelled so loud it echoed through the room and he took off his mask since she'd already blown his cover.

"Where the shit, Shayla?" Malik said calmly.

"This how you do your big sis, nigga? You spend nights over my house with my brother, you was family," she said seriously feeling betrayed because Malik was like family.

When Boss told Malik about robbing Shayla, he was against it because Shayla was a real bitch and he'd known her brother for years.

"It's a cold game. The bitch ain't selling children's books." Boss held a stone face.

90

"Fuck all that family shit, bitch. Where your stash at?" Animal looked around the room impressed that everything was Fendi designed.

"It's all money in the safe in the walk-in closet behind the photo of my momma. The drugs are under the floor under y'all feet, that's all I have," she said flatly upset at herself for slipping on some dick because if she wasn't fucking, she would've seen them coming.

Malik went to the closet on the other side of the room that had everything: a mirror, cabinets, racks, space, and designer bags, shoes, clothes, and everything you can find in a mall.

Animal lifted the cherry oakwood floor panel. "Okay," Animal said, grabbing two large duffle bags from the floor.

Shayla rocked back and forth while Malik walked back into the room with two laundry bags full of money dragging them.

"This bitch was holding," Boss said with his ski mask still on, looking at Shayla's evil face.

"Never go against the grain, Malik! You think you and your crew gonna get away with this?" she yelled crying.

"We Chi-Raq Gangstas, we not a crew, we family," Malik said before shooting her nine times in her face.

Boss and Animal both hit her four times apiece in her chest and the impact knocked her off her bed.

They walked out the front door they'd broken into with a locksmith that they'd brought earlier. It was 4:00 a.m. so they weren't worried about being spotted, as they climbed in a stolen van.

A Week Later

Boss and Animal were leaving a locked park, drained. They spent an hour and a half exercising in the Chicago heat. They did cardio and stomach workouts. Boss was back on his workout shit, it was summertime and he was trying to get right.

"Good looks, bro, I needed that," Boss said as they walked up a hill to their cars.

"Anytime, I love burning niggas up, but that last lick was pretty. I even got a nice little crib out there on one-hundred seventh Street," Animal said.

"That's what's up, Joe. My Uncle got a buyer for all them keys, bro. So, after we split the one-hundred and seventy Ls apiece we should be up. We need to go on a vacation and get out of town or something," Boss said being honest because the city was on fire.

There had been RIP shirts everywhere of Shayla and Big Scoop niggas was taking their death hard.

"Yeah, I agree but Malik got a crew of workers ready to get money from the Satan Disciples in Harvely and Chicago Heights. So, if shit go good with Face and the plan we're gonna have the city on lock," Animal said as he saw a black Toyota coming their way, the two niggas staring at him made him uneasy.

When Boss saw the Dracos rise out of the windows he and Animal pulled out their 9 mms and started busting at the moving car while civilians ran all over the place. The gunmen hopped out of the car, letting shots off at them. The shots from the Draco almost took Boss and Animal legs off as they ran up the hill shooting back hitting one of the gunmen.

"We gotta get out of here," Boss said climbing in his get-around car which was a Honda truck as Animal got in his Ford Explorer.

The civilians helped three civilians who'd got hit in the crossfire and two of them were kids.

The Village

Shaw pulled up into the back of an alley and left the car he rented from a crackhead, so he could do a drill in but it turned out bad. Shaw has been aligned with the crew since the night he dropped off the ransom money for his homie Big Scoop.

That night Shaw awaited in the cut and followed Animal to his home, and he hadn't been on his line since. Today was a perfect day. He planned to kill two birds with one stone but instead, he lost his little cousin H-O at the crime scene with others who lost their innocent lives which is every day in the city.

Shaw was a New Bread and he was into chasing money not beef, but they killed his big homie, so he was on one. At twenty-nine years old he'd seen most of all his family either in the feds or dead. Now he had to go explain to his aunt what happened to her seventeen-year-old son. Shaw was a short, chubby, loud nigga with a bag and a crew of hustlers, but his guys were truly killers. They were all men so Shaw would have to drop a bag on Animal and his guys or put in some pain himself.

Romell Tukes

Chapter 16

United Center

Malik and Face were first row seats at a Bulls and Nets basketball game in the packed arena and the game was almost over with thirty seconds left on the clock. Simone reached out to her cousin Face for her hubby because she knew if he was going to at least get money, it should be with her older cousin who had the city on lock with Heroin supply.

Face was half-African but one could never tell because he was born and raised in the Southside of the city. He'd been in the game for years he was pushing forty-years-old and one of the richest niggas in Chicago. He was very smooth and quiet. He was the type to never expose his hand and he had a lot of pull. He was a Black P Stone Ranger under his old head B. Stone who was a new lieutenant in his drug operation. Face was moving weight in Michigan and Ohio he was big time.

Face Stone is what the guys call him, he was average height, slim, with a long beard, short, dark nappy hair, and he always wore suits. He invested a lot of money into real estate, city projects, construction sites, and youth program centers. He made sure all his guys gave back to the hood as he was taught to do by the older Stones.

"That was a good game," Face said as he and Malik made it out to the parking lot where Face's grey Rolls Royce Phantom was awaiting him.

"Yeah, thanks for bringing me out," Malik said.

"No issue, you're family. When Simone hollered at me, I didn't mind because you're a good dude. So, doing business with you is my pleasure, I can care less how you get the money," he said looking at him. "But first we have a little problem." Face stopped near his Rolls Royce.

"Problem?" Malik wondered if he'd gotten one of Face's people, if so, he would leave him and his bodyguard right there in the lot.

Face's bodyguard and personal driver was 6'7 and three-hundred and sixty pounds of solid muscle. He looked like he could snap a nigga's neck without any pressure.

"I'm a very connected man. I have people in the Chicago PD. Your name has come up in a murder but the only thing that connects you to the murder is one person," Face informed.

Malik had a dumb look on his face. "Who?"

"You know Rico Knowles?" Face asked.

Malik's head sank and his stomach. "That's my little cousin."

"You can't even trust family these days. But now you know the situation. When you handle your situation we can begin our situation," Face instructed hopping in his Rolls Royce as his guard opened the door and got him.

When he pulled off, Malik was pissed. He couldn't believe his little cousin crossed lines and crossed him, family or not Malik had to do something.

Four Weeks Later

Shaw was on his way home from the strip club, something he did every weekend. He liked this club, and he enjoyed tricking off with the dancers. Lately, however, his fun time had been limited because his trap had been raided by the police and he had lost 22 kilos and $550,000. Besides, fretting over the huge loss, Shaw had been busy with the responsibility of bailing his workers out of jail, the ones who had been arrested during the raid.

He was driving a white Porsche 918 Spyder, he stopped at a red light near the brickyard sections in K-Town. When the light turned green, a green and black Corvette ZR1 pulled up to his side. Shaw was so tipsy he couldn't even focus on the road normally he wanted to leave with his crew, but they were still in the strip club.

Bloc! Bloc! Bloc! Bloc! Bloc!

Animal shot Shaw in his neck twice and his upper chest as the Porsche crashed into a light pole. Animal spun off on his way back to the Southside. Animal remembered Shaw's face the day at the park from the Big Scoop lick, he'd been gone for a while so he didn't know who he was so he went to speak to Jenny. He asked her about seeing him and all she could tell him was that she heard he likes to trick at the strip clubs at least that's what Kimmie told her a while back. He had a feeling Shaw was going to be at the hottest clubs in the city if he wanted to catch him and just as he guessed, Shaw and his crew were there.

When Animal saw his crew, he thought he may have needed an extra hand but when he saw him leave alone and tipsy, he knew it was his time.

Buff City

Fame was in his homie's crib on 100 Perry Street a.k.a Dirty Perry surrounded by guns and drugs. Last night, the Fame's soldier was going through some shit, she was crying about how had to bury her favorite cousin. Fame tried to explain to her it was a lie then got some head and pussy but shawty was crying and acting too emotional for his taste.

She explained to him how she was in the next step when she heard the commotion, she went into everyday step by step basically forcing him to listen. When she said the name Chi'Raq Gangstas she caught his full attention. Fame knew niggas got robbed every day, but this was too similar to Loso and Big Scoop. The name Chi'Raq Gangstas rang a bell in his head. He heard the name before while in prison, but the name Malik was new to him.

Fame was doing his research on this Malik dude and the Chi'Raq Gangstas because there was no doubt in his mind, they were responsible for his best friend's murder.

103rd Police Station

Malik was parked down the block from the police station behind Rico's car watching him walk out of the police station. Malik regretted he didn't see the signs that he had rats and snakes. He saw Rico walking up to his car in his rearview mirror and he rolled his window down.

"Rico—" Malik said.

Rico almost jumped out of his skin as if he saw a ghost. "Oh, shit Malik. What's up, cuz, what you doing here? I just got arrested for a bench warrant, but they gave me a ticket and a court date," Rico spoke fast.

"A'ight—hop in, I got a lick for us across town."

"My mom waiting on me, you know how she is."

"Come on this will be a quick, fam," Malik said.

Rico really had no choice, so he got in the Nissan. They drove around for a while talking and catching up as Malik pulled up to a nice neighborhood on Maryland Road in front of a two-story house.

"What did you say to those people?" Malik said, pulling out a gun, placing it on his lap.

Rico got nervous. "Just about the Big Scoop shit, cuz. I'm sorry I had caught a gun charge but they needed me to get you on wire saying you killed them people in the drive-thru."

"That's all?"

"Yeah, because they don't have nothing on y'all. The cameras was down that night at McDonald's and y'all had on masks but I can fix this, cuz."

"You did enough, Rico."

"I know, I'm sorry I wasn't going to go all the way with it."

"Rico, stop please."

"Just let me fix—"

Boc! Boc! Boc!

Malik shot Rico in his new era cap and shoved his body out of his car onto the lawn before pulling off. Since Face told him about Rico, he'd been on his tail meeting with detectives and police daily, at all hours. Malik had to do something because one bad apple could eventually spoil it for everybody.

Malik didn't even tell Boss or Animal about this because it was something, he had to take care of himself. He knew how the home-owners came out in the morning, so somebody was going to be in for a surprise.

98

Chi'Raq Gangstas

Chapter 17

87ᵗʰ and Jeffery

Fame watched Malik's sister Jasmine like a hawk as she walked around the block looking over her shoulders in a nice, tight dress showing her nice, round breasts and curves wearing six-inch high heels. When she got inside the new, black Lexus LC 500 Coupe with tints, he smiled from behind the wheel of his Yukon truck and followed her, with his gun in hand.

The other day Fame was in Bluff City with his goons, shooting dice in an alley on L Block when his little homie Spazz O pulled up with a sexy, high-yellow bitch. Fame asked who she was, he told him she was his wife, when he asked her where she was from, he told him Jeffory Street.

Fame made a statement about him being on the VLs turf looking for that, but Spazz O told him her whole family was Vice Lords and her brother's name was Malik. When he heard the name Malik, he played it cool and watched him closely.

Spazz O had no clue what Fame was planning. He didn't know he was being followed by Fame and his soldiers. He had his head so far stuck up Jasmine's ass that he couldn't see past it.

As the Lexus' tail lights dazed down the city streets at 8:00 p.m. Fame stayed a close distance, wondering where the night was going to lead but Fame planned to send Malik a message one way or another.

Spazz O pulled into Limelight Cinema movie theater's parking lot so they could catch a new funny movie that just came out with Kevin Hart.

"I hope I can focus on the movie with you looking like that," Spazz O said, looking at her phat ass through his Cartier frames.

"You so nasty, but maybe I can give you a little treat until later," she said holding his hand as they entered the large movie theater to wait in line to pay for tickets.

Spazz O was a BD, but he was more of the pretty boy type and into fashion and money, he was a big-time scammer. He was tall, dark, and lean, with braids, tats on his face, and he wore diamonds in his mouth, around the neck and his wrists. They were both dressed to stunt tonight, he wore a Balmain outfit and she wore a Balmain dress with her hair done in a bun and a little make-up.

They'd met six months ago in Lange, Downtown. Jasmine loved dark, handsome niggas. Spazz O was all that in one and he had a bag. Jasmine led him to the top corner of the theater as the movie began and people started yelling for niggas to be quiet. Twenty-five minutes into the movie, Spazz O's mind focused on something else and he put his finger inside her wetness. She came on his finger twice, while trying hard to hold back her moans.

She couldn't take it no more, she lowered her head into his lap and unbuckled his Gucci belt, pulled out his nice size dick, and engulfed him. Jasmine bopped her head up and down taking him deep into her throat almost choking twice while she fingered herself and tried to suck the black off his dick. When he nutted, she spit it on the floor because she didn't swallow, she disliked the salty, nasty taste of a nigga's cum.

"Let's get a hotel, I saw one on the way here. Fuck this movie, we can catch it on Netflix," Jasmine said horny as hell.

"We out," Spazz O said, glad she read his mind.

They left the movie theater and drove to a cheap hotel a few blocks away with its light on. Spazz O paid for the room in a rush as the lady at the front desk shook her head, disgusted from seeing horny, nasty, young kids all day, leaving used condoms, dirty tampons, dirty panties, and bloody clothes everywhere for the maid to clean. Once they were in room 171 the couple got comfortable, ready to finish what they started.

"I'ma take a shower real quick. You better get that nigga up before I get back," she said walking into the bathroom undressing. Her thick thighs jiggled, and her phat ass bounced like basketballs on her way into the shower.

Spazz O turned on the hotel TV and the news was on, he heard a knock on the door.

"Who the fuck is it?" Spazz O yelled going to open the door.

Four guys stood there with evil looks.

"What's up?" Spazz O said as Fame and his goons walked inside the room, hearing the shower running from the bathroom.

"Where she at?" Fame asked.

Spazz O closed the door and became uneasy wondering how they even found him. "Who—what you talking about?" Spazz O said.

Fame pulled out a gun, pointed it at his head, and blew his brains out.

The shower turned off. "Spazz—Chris!" Jasmine yelled hearing a loud thump in the room and she jumped out of the shower naked.,

Jasmine ran into the room to see four guns aimed at her and Spazz O laying in a puddle of blood with a hole in his head the size of a pancake.

"Grab her," Fame told his goons.

They rushed her and pinned her to the wall as she tried to scream and fight, but it was useless.

"Calm down, I just want to know where I can find your brother," Fame said standing over her body looking at her big, bald pussy that looked like a wallet filled with money.

"I don't know where he is. I haven't seen him in months. Please just let me go, I don't want to die," she cried.

"Tell me where he is then you can go home and forget about everything that happened tonight." Fame was running out of patience.

"I swear I don't know where he is!"

"A'ight buss her down then kill her," Fame said, stepping over Spazz O's body as he walked out.

His guys began raping Jasmine in her pussy and ass as she cried and screamed in pain bleeding everywhere, then they shot her to death.

Lake Shore Drive

Boss bought Rosie a nice condo downtown away from the hood, so they could live a more comfortable life. The area was beautiful and mainly for the upper-class type, so Rosie was overwhelmed.

The condo had marble, white floors, a floating, glass staircase leading to the second level, a Jacuzzi, two terraces, five bedrooms, four walk-in bathrooms, it was 12,172 square feet, with two stone fireplaces, a spacious gym downstairs, an indoor pool and a private bar area.

"I love this place. I'ma put the finishing touches on it this weekend," Rosie said walking into the living room where Boss was watching the very large flat-screen TV that took up half the living room wall.

"This your home," he said standing and walking over to the balcony to see the city's beautiful skyline that shined at night-time.

"Our our home, baby," she corrected leaning on the rail as Boss got on one knee. "Boy, you not about to eat my pussy out here," she said then she saw a box.

"Will you marry me, Rosie de Anna Lopez?" Boss said.

Her face went black when she saw the big ass rock. "Oh, my God, Boss! You really doing this? Oh, my God! Of course, I will. Nigga is you crazy? Yes!" she screamed as tears ran down her face.

Rosie fucked Boss on the terrace, in the living room, kitchen, shower, patio, dining room table and they made love for hours then talked until the early morning hours.

Two Weeks Later

Malik was sitting on the front row at his sister's funeral shedding tears behind his Louis Vuitton shades with his man on the side of him going through it. Boss and Animal were in the second row showing support. The church was packed with friends and family. When Malik heard about his sister's death, he went crazy ready to kill the whole city, but he couldn't until he found out who was behind this.

He wouldn't have believed six years ago that he would be burying his little sister. The police told his mom that before she was killed, she was badly raped. They assured her they would find the killers, but everyone knew that Chicago Police were lazy and didn't give a fuck about murders. Malik was on a serious manhunt for Jasmine's killer. He paused his life to get even and his crew was behind him.

Chapter 18

Southside, Chi-Town

Detective Rodriguez rode around the city on his way to the Westside to speak to Rico's family to see if they could help him make sense of his death. The thing that fucked Rodriguez head up the most was how Rico's killer tossed his body on his lawn. When Rodriquez woke up to take out his trash as he did every other morning, he saw nats and flies crawling all over Rico's dead body. Rodriguez was a little shaken up because the killer knew where he lived, and it was obvious they knew who he was and his deal with Rico.

Malik was the first person to come to mind but if he was to build a case on him it would be weak and worthless because his star witness and rat was dead, now he had to go another route. Rodriquez saw Lil' BD and Hitler on the corner pistol-whipping a crackhead but he kept going as if he didn't see anything.

Boss walked into his Uncle's building in his all-white Gucci attire because he had plans to go out clubbing a little late with the guys, but Malik was on him.

Since his sister's death, he'd been acting a little off, but Boss understood because any time you lose someone very close it would normally take a while to snap back. His Uncle called him explaining that he had to see him asap and Boss already had a clue what it was about.

When Boss reached his uncle's building, he took the stairs up. As he ascended the steps, he heard a woman's voice.

"I know what I was sent to do. Look, it takes time. I'll call you when I'm ready, put yourself in my shoes," she was saying.

Boss walked up the stairs to see Carolina his Uncle's new whore. She was frozen for a second wondering how long he'd been there as she looked at him with her sparkly eyes.

"Hey," she said sexily.

He nodded his head. "I'm Carolina, I saw you around here before. You must be somebody special. If you need something just ask we can keep it between us," she said looking at his handsome face.

"I don't do hookers or hoes," he said.

She frowned and stormed off down the stairs.

A minute later, Boss knocked on his uncle's door and was let inside.

"Nephew, what's popping," Uncle Jay said, eating a hamburger.

Boss walked inside thinking about Carolina's conversation on the phone.

"What you got for me?"

"Lil' Moe the Four Corner Hustler nigga from one-o-seven Champlain."

"That's where all the Four's at. You trying to get a nigga killed that's where he be at. Besides on 68th and Dorchester, I believe he got a BM that lives somewhere over there from my understanding."

"What kinda car does he drive?" Boss was trying to make some sense of the situation.

"A sky-blue Lamborghini Huracan."

"I saw that shit recently somewhere." Boss remembered.

"He got a brother named, Canon. He's the king cobra snake and dangerous like poison so you gotta be smart because if he gets wind it's going to be bad, Joe."

"A'ight I'll get up with you when it's handled, but I got a question. How well do you know these women you be pimping? Do you be doing background checks?" Boss said.

His uncle looked at him as if he was crazy. "All my hoes are top of the line. Why you ask? If you want some pussy nephew just ask. I see the way you be looking at my hoes," he said with a smirk.

Boss shook his head and walked toward the door. "A'ight—" Boss said leaving and texting Malik so they could meet on the weekend to discuss the new lick.

Meanwhile

Malik inhaled deep from his blunt of purple kush as he tried to relax his nerves while he watched Fame's parent's house on block 109th Street in Buff City.

106

Thanks to Animal he was able to find everything out about Fame except where he lived because Animal believed he'd moved to the city. His parent's house was enough to make him feel the pain he felt over his little sister's death. He'd just received a text from Boss on his smartphone saying they needed to talk at the regular location.

He texted back. *//: Copy, bro, love!*

Malik grabbed his Draco and ski mask then thought against the ski mask because he wanted them to see his face before he drilled them. Montana was Fame's mother, a fifty-two-year-old, brown-skinned, skinny, grayed haired woman. Her husband was a little younger at forty-five-years-old.

"That's the doorbell love," Montana told Mel as he stood up from the couch watching the Snowfall TV show.

Mel didn't expect company this late, but he figured, maybe his wife had some family coming over. He didn't feel like being bothered.

When he opened the door, he quickly wished he hadn't.

Boom!

The powerful Draco ripped through his face like a sword. Malik stepped inside just as Montana jumped over the couch and ran toward the kitchen. He caught her by the back of her gown and slammed her to the floor exposing her bushy pussy.

"What is going on? I'm an old woman," she cried, but Malik was unsympathetic. He was on a cold, heartless mission that could not be thwarted.

A crazy look was in his eyes, Malik pulled down his pants and got between her frail legs, forcing them open. She tried to fight him until he slapped the shit out of her and cruelly rammed his dick inside of her.

"No! Please don't!" Montana screamed feeling him ripping her inner lining.

"Shut the fuck up!"

Malik flipped her on her stomach and roughly began sodomizing her.

The woman screamed out in pain. To silence her, he ruthlessly shot her in the back of the head execution-style.

Chapter 19

Lincoln Park Southside

The Chi'Raq Gangstas all stood in a circle in the dark park on the basketball court and the night had a windy breeze outside.

"Is everybody cool with this shit," Boss said.

"Yeah, he is a Four Corner hustler. So, he should be easy to get at because the niggas be all around the city," Malik said sipping lean out of a big white cup.

"We ain't got him on his block. The Fours got that whole shit sewed up, bro," Boss said trying to come up with a plan because he couldn't afford no slips up at least not now.

"I got a plan." Animal spoke up.

'What?" Boss asked.

He and Malik looked at Animal's evil grin.

"Just follow my lead. Malik you are going to be on standby to catch the bag when we give you the call," Animal instructed.

Malik nodded his head. "Are you sure about this?"

"Boss, chill just give me a couple of days and be ready when I call," Animal said.

"A'ight. Yo' Malik you good, bro? I heard what happened to your little cousin, bro," Boss said.

Malik showed no remorse. "He got jammed up out here, he knew what he was getting himself into,"Malik said coldly.

They just looked at him. Malik never told them Rico was a rat and he killed him because he didn't want the guys to question his loyalty or think he was down with it since he brought him in.

"What happened with Fame's situation? I told you we can pause and take care of this goofy nigga," Boss said.

"Nah, I'ma wait. We gonna continue to do us, I'ma handle him soon, first I gotta meet with Face."

"A'ight, Joe, I just don't want bad timing to backfire," Boss said.

"I heard niggas killed his parents," Animal said looking at Malik, his face told it all. He didn't mention the part about his mom being raped.

"Damn, Malik, you colder than I thought, bro. Just keep your eyes open, I'll holla at y'all," Boss said leaving as they split up.

Days Later: Beacon Hills

Lil Moe was on the block full of run-down, boarded-up row houses and foreclosed homes all connected as the 4's trapped in the abandoned buildings making thousands a day.

"Lil Moe, I'ma need two birds tomorrow. That work you had the block going crazy and looking like a block party for a week straight," Deuce told him, he was leaning on his Lambo counting a few blue faces and his long dreads covered his big, apple-shaped head.

"I'ma have the guys drop it off to you. I'ma shootout to Atlanta tonight, me and Pick 4. So, I'm be gone for a couple of days, Joe." Lil Moe looked down the block to see fiends arguing as hustlers passed off drugs to other friends coming and going.

Lil Moe was a Four Corner Hustler gang member. His crew was into selling drugs and scamming all across the Midwest. At twenty-years-old, he was seeing big bucks thanks to his father who was a plug in Atlanta. He was short at 5'5, with long tan, brown dreads, and tattoos all over his face, even his eyelids were tatted. He had a baby face but that's where people would get him confused until he let the wolves out. Nobody played with Lil Moe because of his brother Canon. He was a snake gang member, and he was one of the deadliest niggas on the Westside.

Pick 4 finally came out on the block with a bag full of money. It was today's profit on the block. Lil Moe had five blocks doing numbers on dope, coke, PCP, and molly he was the man.

"You ready, bro?" Pick 4 said tossing the money into the Lambo and taking a deep breath not because he was overweight but inside Lil Moe's workers were bagging and cutting dope and the smell was so strong it sticks to your skin.

Lil Mac and Pick 4 were both dressed in Dolce & Gabbana outfits with Cuban link chains and bust down Rolexes.

"We out, tell the guys I'll be back in a couple of days. And Pick 4," Lil Moe said climbing into the sky-blue Lambo. "We gotta go to Chicago Heights to pick up some more money, then we can bounce."

"I can't wait, it's been a while since we got away, bro." Pick 4 placed his hand on Lil Moe's upper thigh.

"Like that when I'm driving," Lil Moe said, smiling as Pick 4 leaned in and pulled out his small dick.

"Just like that," Pick 4 said, wrapping his thick lips around his dick, deepthroating it, and taking it back and forth down his throat with ease until he nutted all over his face. He sucked him dry while Lil Moe's toes curled in his designer shoes as he tried to focus on the main streets.

Lil Moe and Pick 4 were gay gangsters just like a lot gang banger in the city even though niggas was in the closet they still got down. They would go to Atlanta to have guy orgies with niggas they would meet in clubs since Atlanta's gay population was number one in the world, then they would re-up from Lil Moe's pops who was also a faggot.

"Wait until we get to Atlanta," Lil Moe said.

"I'm not doing that shit we did last time. Taking two dicks up my ass. I was hurting for a week," Pick 4 said seriously, and Lil Moe laughed.

"Nah, I got something else in mind."

"Okay, I'm down," Pick 4 said as blue flashing lights on a Crown Vic were on the bumper behind him.

He pulled out a Glock with a *glizzy* from the stash compartment inside the passenger seat which was noticeable even if one was stolen.

Lil Moe pulled over and rolled down his window with his ID and License ready. Pick 4 placed the money he'd just picked up under his seat.

Lil Moe was unable to see the cops face as he approached both windows and he tried to wipe the cum stain off his black Dolce Gabbana jeans.

Boc! Boc! Boc! Boc! Boc!

Pick 4's head flew off his shoulders, Lil Moe was so shook he screamed like a bitch as the other man snatched him from the car dragging him into the truck. The two men that toss back into the truck wore FBI uniforms. Halfway down the block Lil Moe came to the conclusion that these niggas weren't cops because they were young and playing Lil Jay Clout Boyz mixtape in the loudspeakers as they drove to Southside.

The truck pulled into an alley which was pitched dark and in the cut. The car turned off and the driver faced Lil Moe holding him at gunpoint.

"Where is your stash spot, Lil Moe, and I'ma ask you once," Boss said.

Lil Moe said nothing. *Boc!* Boss shot him in his knee cap. "Ahhhhh!" Lil Moe yelled.

Animal punched him in the face three times.

"I think you are ready now," Boss said as he gave Animal a look to let go because he was about to kill him before they even got the money and drugs.

"Sixty-eight and Dorchester," Lil Moe said, trying to breathe.

"Who's there and don't lie?"

"A man stays there. The safe is in the cooler in the kitchen under some food, the code is 2-17-41-4," Lil Moe said.

Boss extended everything to Malik who was already parked on Dorchester.

"Building number and apartment number?"

"Build 61 and 6B," he said trying to remain strong knowing niggas get robbed every day, but he had no enemies. The only nigga he could think of was Jay because he fronted the old head one and a half keys of dope and never saw him again. To find out he owed the whole city big money.

"You okay, sorry about your man back there he was moving funny," Animal said laughing catching a glance at the fresh cum stain on his pants.

"What the fuck is that?" Animal asked, looking at Lil Moe's frog eyes.

"Bird shit. Did old Jay send y'all?" he said catching Boss's attention.

"Why would you ask that?" Boss replied.

"That nigga owes me a lot of money. He owed Shaya, Sin G, Big Scoop, and almost every big hitter in the city," Lil Moe said.

Boss's mind started racing because his Uncle had been playing him this whole time. No wonder he knew so many details about the victims, Boss was pissed.

68th and Dorchester

Malik was looking for apartment 6B which was at the end of the hallway, once he received Boss's text it was easy to find the spot; he was parked two apartment buildings next to it. Malik had no choice but to knock but first, he looked under the mat to see if there was a spare key, an old trick he learned years ago living in the PJs. To his surprise the was a key there, he used it to get inside the apartment, which was clean, nice, and had new furniture, new carpet, smelled good, and TVs everywhere.

Malik went to check on Lil Moe's hoe that was there. He crept down the hallway with his pistol and heard Avant playing loud in the first room. Malik knew whoever was in there had a bitch in there and was giving him the business.

Boom! Malik kicked the door in and saw the craziest shit he'd ever seen. Fame was fucking a skinny nigga from behind pounding his guts out, as the skinny nigga's sex faces changed with every stroke until Malik stopped the party. Malik was shocked he'd finally caught up with Fame, the man who had carried a picture around in his wallet.

"What you gonna do homie?" Fame said sitting on the bed ass naked while the punk tried to hide behind him.

"I have nothing to do with this, so um you can let me go cutie," the gay nigga said rolling his dick trying to get out of view of the gun Malik had that looked like it could take a nigga's arm off.

Boom! Boom! Boom!

Malik killed the gay nigga, Fame showed no emotion. He'd just met that nigga two nights ago but his head game and ass was good. Fame knew he had a man that was going out of town. That's why he came by for a quickie but if he'd known this would happen he would've laid low like he'd been doing since he lost his parents.

"I was at war with a homo thug?" Malik spat.

"You do a lot of time behind the walls in prison, you're chasing ass too," Fame said before Malik shot him in the head three times.

He went to the safe and punched in the code after moving frozen food. When the safe unlocked he was at a loss of words.

Lil Moe explained to Boss what his Uncle was on and Boss knew it was true because it all made sense now. When Malik texted him, he smiled and shot Lil Moe twenty times before leaving him in the alleyway then headed on his way to meet Malik.

Chapter 20

Las Vegas, NV: Weeks Later

Boss and Rosie were in a Rolls Royce limousine on their way to get married. As they looked out of the window of the bright Vegas nightlife, they saw big, beautiful hotels and casinos, and hookers walked up and down the 1 ½ mile strip trying to grab a tourist.

"Baby, you look so beautiful," Boss said looking at the white Ralph Lauren dress she was wearing.

"You look okay," she said laughing and fixing his tie on his Emporio Armani suit, he also wore his new Audemars Piguet watch.

They both made the choice to get married and have their honeymoon in Vegas. Rosie wanted a small wedding and what's smaller than getting married in Vegas? The lick from Lil Moe put the crew up in 42 keys and close to a half of a million. Boss made the choice to cut his uncle out of the deal because he was playing them the whole time, he was lucky he didn't kill him.

When Malik told Boss how he caught Fame fucking the punk, he was shocked he had no clue. When Lil' Moe said his man was there he had no clue that was his real man. Animal found the story so fucked up he almost cried but they were happy Fame was now out of the picture at least.

"You ready to embark on a whole new level?" Boss asked wifey as the limo stopped in front of a small Chapel with big bright lights that said, *Get Married.*

'Yes, baby."

"You sure you wanna do it like this, boo? We can do it big if you want."

"No, this is perfect. I'm not that type of chick. You know none of that material shit can't buy love. Now let's go get married," Rosie said as Boss got out opening doors like a true gentleman.

An hour later, they were married in the state of Nevada. They then went to the most expensive hotel in Vegas, they had the penthouse suite which was on the 38th Floor with its own roof helipad, pool, outside bar, party area, and a view of Vegas. Inside was majestic status with three levels, a pirate lounge, bars on each level, a glass elevator, very small glass fountains, and covered fireside family rooms on each level. Baldwin bronze marble tiles, climate control, a hot tub in the patio, and it was large for hosting events on the roof pad. A club room, a movie theater, an 80-foot ceiling, 17,917 square feet, five bedrooms, and three bathrooms. The place looked more like a penthouse suite.

Boss and his wife stripped down and climb into a rooftop Jacuzzi, naked with a bottle of Dom P and some fire exotic weed they'd bought earlier from a cannabis shop.

"I love you so much, baby. But now that I am married, I believe we need to have this task. I want to have a family and not have to worry about being a single mother out there. So, how long do you need a plan?" she said closing in on him between his legs and rubbing her breasts on his chest as she listened.

"To be honest I don't have a legit plan. I'm just trying to stack this bread, boo. I'll let you come up with a legit plan as far as how long I'ma be in the field. To be honest, until me and all my guys get rich," he said.

She nodded her head respecting his honesty. "It's time for my meds," she said, going underwater to suck his dick.

Boss ain't want her to pass out while sucking his dick underwater, so he sat on the edge of the pool and she got between his legs. He acted nonchalant about her head game but for real she would have a nigga crying for his mama. She wrapped her thick lips around his head, slowly taking him inch by inch into her warm mouth.

"Mmmmm," he moaned, watching her work as she increased her speed making it wet and sloppy just as he liked.

Boss guided her head up and down as his pre-cum dripped from her mouth.

"You that good, babe, fuck my face," she moaned holding his dick in her mouth as he thrust his hips and pelvis into her face driving his dick to the back of her throat until he reached his peak. When he nutted, she swallowed it all. "Ummmm, I love it, babe," she said smiling.

Boss pressed her against the Jacuzzi and lifted her in the water while entering her tight wet pussy at the same time, she grabbed his broad shoulders for balance.

"Uuuuhhhh shiddd, papi!" she let out a loud yelp as he went deep into her tightness, she screamed out his name grinding on his dick. "I'm cumminggg, babe!" she yelled, nutting on his dick as he came with her.

They got out of the pool and raced inside naked to the master bedroom and Rosie ended up beating him. She won so she wanted to ride him. As she positioned his dick, it took a second for his dick to enter her tight love box. He rapidly guided her up and down and she started jumping up and down on the dick.

"Fu-c-c-k-k-k! Yesss!" she yelled breathing hard as he sucked on her nipples and breasts.

After they climaxed, he turned her around to see the tiger in her eyes, she was in her sex zone just as he was. Boss bent her over and gripped her waist with both hands as she toted her ass in the air, and he rubbed the tip of his dick in her wet dripping pussy.

He stroked inside her, gradually picking up his pace, and made his way deeper into her. She arched her back wanting it all in her.

"Fuck this good pussy, papi."

"Take it." He grabbed her ponytail, cocking her head back with one hand, and slapping her ass with his free hand, ramming his dick in her harder.

"Like that, yesss!" she yelled rotating her hips trying to throw her ass back, he was killing her shit. "I'm cumming, don't stop!" she yelled.

"You about to make me nut too," he moaned, stroking faster as her pussy walls got tight, clenching his dick and they both climaxed hard again. She had cum squirting out her pussy this was the first time she ever squirted so hard.

"Damn," Boss said, cheesing and seeing puddles of semen everywhere.

Rosie cocked her legs open so he could eat her small, pretty pussy, and perfectly folded vagina lips made for sucking. Boss sucked and licked her clit until she came hard, then she wanted him to fuck in her ass, anal wasn't her thing but tonight it was. Boss fucked her slowly in her backdoor until he got her loose then he worked hard into the morning hours.

Downtown, Chi-Town

Animal was in a five-star restaurant with Chole who was dressed in a black, Versace, satin chess with her hair down her back. Animal wore a Prada suit to look like a true gentleman to impress her because she was on another level. Animal finally called her a couple of days ago since they'd met in the designer store. She haunted his mind, but he had to force himself to wait until he got his life in order as he did now. Animal was finally up thanks to Lil Moe. He was sitting on a nice piece of change, his wrists, ears, fingers, and neck were iced out, he was a big jewelry fine.

"Tell me more about you, DeWayne," Chole asked, eating a seafood tray while sipping wine.

"I told you about everything. Ask me something?"

"Have you made better choices and decisions since you were out?" she asked, looking him into his eyes.

"I have a lot, I never really had a plan until now. So, I'm focused on making my goals and plans come together in one."

"That's good, as you know we have a big age gap. How do you feel about that?"

"I should be asking you that. You see all these niggas in here staring over here. I'm sure they not staring at me," he said making her laugh.

"I see, but I've told you I'm a busy woman with a busy life, my job takes up a lot of my time."

"What is it that you do again?"

"I own an industrial engineering company," she said, drinking some more wine.

He ate his lobster rice and fancy grilled chicken with fried veggies on top of the chicken. "Okay, whenever you can make time, I'm all for it."

"Good. Now, are you involved with anybody at the moment? If so, let me know so I won't get in my feelings. If we do get serious because I really like you, DeWayne. When I first laid eyes on you after you walk into the store that day, you did something to me. My family is Colombian, I was born in Bogota. You rarely see sexy, black men, it's mostly Spanish. Growing up in Chicago I took a liking to dark men with a gangsta side," she said with a chuckle. "I want to know I will be all yours."

"Only a fool wouldn't treasure you. Chloe you're the most beautiful women I've seen since I've been on earth. Yesterday was my birthday. I was in a club when you texted me to meet you here. I didn't even look at the dancers."

"They must've been some ugly dancers?"

"Some of them," he replied truthfully, and she laughed.

They enjoyed the rest of their night. Then later, in the parking lot, she gave him a kiss on the lips and hopped in her Bentley.

"There is a lot you will learn about me. I hope we can learn about each other. I'm sure we have a lot to offer each other," she said before driving off.

Animal couldn't wait to taste her insides.

Romell Tukes

Chapter 21

Buff City

Lil' BD left O-Block walking to the new Cadillac CTs, it was midnight and dark out to his surprise the block wasn't lit right. He'd just come from chilling with some black hoes, that he called sisters and the guys. He left Hitler with the gang because he was gone off the syrup. Tonight again, Lil BD and Hitler caught a big sting for 30K, and a half of key and some pill networked at street value for 22K which they flipped the next day.

The Vic G-Baby was a well-known GD from Southeast on Longley Street. They killed him as he was coming out of one of the GD hangouts, Hitler took off with the pack without getting hit up.

Lil' BD wore a Louis Vuitton vest and Ray Bane jeans. He was heading home since his mom called him earlier informing him that she'd left a plate of food for him in the oven and he was starving.

It was warm and quiet outside, but Lil' BD felt as if someone was watching him, lately he'd been extra cautious. At the drop of a dime, Lil' BD turned around to see two gunmen barefaced racing his way trying to snake him. He pulled out but he wasn't fast enough, shots quickly waved past his head.

Bloc! Bloc! Bloc! Bloc! Bloc! Bloc!

Lil' BD bust shots as the car alarm went off and sirens could be heard from a close distance. The gunman took off running down the block as he heard the sirens. Lil' BD ran down the block to see a car pull up on him, he thought he was about to die until he saw that it was a woman.

"Get in, BD, hurry," Jenny said, pulling up on him in her Infiniti Q60.

She was coming out of her mom's house to see Lil' BD in action, putting in work. She'd gone to middle school and high school with him. They had all the same classes but he was very quiet. Even though they both knew the same people they never said two words to each other.

Lil BD saw it was Jenny and hopped in her car, she made a left and a right on her way to Chapel Street where her new crib she recently got two weeks ago was thanks to some big scams she did in Iowa.

"Shit, I think I'm hit!" he yelled clutching his shoulder, he was leaking blood all over his Ray Bane jeans.

"Don't do that shit on my seat, nigga," she said pulling into the back lot of her apartment complex.

Once in the nice apartment, she told him to take off his vest while she went to get band-aids, wraps, alcohols, and some pain killers from her bathroom. When she walked back into the living room and dining room area, she almost lost track of what she was doing when she saw his chiseled six-pack, big chest, tattoos, and grown man arms.

"You're gonna let me bleed to death," he said as she just stood there.

"Here let me help, this may hurt," she said, pouring alcohol on his wounds.

He moaned as she took a warm rag and cleaned off the blood to see that he'd only gotten grazed and not shot.

"Thank you, Jenny," he said looking into her eyes she was always bad but now she looked better than ever.

He hadn't seen her in years, word was that she was fucking around with a basketball nigga and was off in college.

"Sure, I think you should chill here for a while. You know you killed that, nigga?" she said.

"I know. Can I trust you?"

"Don't disrespect me like that," she said seriously as she went to the closet to get him a new t-shirt, luckily, she had a new pack of V-Necks.

"I don't want your boyfriend to pop up then I gotta smoke his ass."

"Boy, please, I'm single and don't mind me," she said pissed off thinking about Pete who was recently murdered. She went to get tested after she caught him cheating and luckily, she didn't have STDs or HIV.

122

"A'ight," he said looking at her curves in her jeans and her ass. She saw him watching her, so she swayed her hips a little hard as she walked.

"You can have my guest room and the bathroom is to the left make sure you lift the toilet," she said laughing and walking to her room.

"Jenn?"

"Yeah."

"I know we never talked in school but thank you for what you just did."

"No, problem. You remember in seventh grade? It was Valentine's Day, and everybody brought all the popular girls gifts in class except me. Then when I went to my locker roses were falling out with chocolate candy and teddy bears," she said smiling thinking back.

"Oh, I don't remember that."

"Well, I knew that was you because the janitor said he saw you break into my locker earlier that morning," she said. He frowned because he'd always wanted to keep that a secret. "That day bitches were all mad and hating on me, so thanks," she said walking off.

Lil' BD texted his mom telling her he was staying across town and he loved her. He knew his mom didn't go to sleep until he came home or checked in with her. Plus, he was a momma boy.

The next morning Jenny woke up in her king-size bed as the sun from outside shined in her room. She smelled cooked food she'd forgotten that Lil BD was there. So, she went to her private bathroom, brushed her teeth, and fixed her hair. She made her way into her living room to see it was clean and to see Lil BD standing over the stainless-steel stove cooking.

"I made you some breakfast, pancakes, eggs, sausages, fresh orange juice, and fruit," he said, not even looking behind him as he finished.

"Wow," she said because no nigga had ever cooked for her. This said a lot about his character.

"Wow, what nigga? I'm sorry I woke you," he said bringing their plates to the dining room table where she was sitting. "This place is nice," he said looking at the long white carpet and walls, a large china cabinet, high ceilings, balcony, a TV above a fireplace, walk-in closets, and a personal office room connected to a guest room.

"Thanks—ummmm, this tastes good," she said as he watched her, she laughed. *"What!"*

"Nothing. What you been up to? I haven't seen you since JaJa's funeral a couple years back," Lil' BD said.

"Facts, I've been focused on college and some other shit, chasing a bag. How about you I see you still be in the hood," she said flatly.

"I do but that shit's dead now because a lot of the guys be on some funny shit. I got plans I was just waiting on my time,"

"You almost got killed, Justin. You gotta move smarter and focus on you. Guys don't care it's every man for themselves out here, bro," she said, and he agreed.

They enjoyed breakfast until Lil' BD had to go. They exchanged numbers and promised to link up soon.

Uncle Jay was pacing back and forth in his crib waiting on his company to arrive, it had been weeks since he'd heard from Boss after he put him on the Lil Moe lick. Uncle Jay saw on the news how his body was found in an alley somewhere, so he knew Boss had to have found the stash. Boss changed his number which made him mad because he let his nephew play with him, but he was going to get him back by any means.

"Come on in!" Uncle Jay yelled.

A tall, dark-skinned nigga waked in wearing all red with short dreads and a gold grill looking like a down South nigga.

"Dirty good to see you, homie, long time no speak," he said with a fake smile but Dirty wasn't smiling.

Dirty was a top-ranking Vice Lord in the city but he was down South running a big drug ring through four states. Dirty's little sister was Shayla and he heard a crew who call themselves Chi'Raq Gangstas was responsible for his sister's death and Malik a nigga he knew well.

"Who are they?"

"Let's talk about money first. The word on the streets is you got fifty-K on the head, but I need seventy-K," Uncle Jay said.

Dirty pulled out a gun and placed it in his face. "How about I just kill you?" he said.

Uncle Jay gulped a ball of spit thinking fast because he knew Dirty wasn't the type to play games.

"Okay, I know who they are, at least the main nigga. His name is Boss. I supply him with hoes, and he pillow talks so he told my hoe's how he runs the crew and he told them about him killing Shayla he's from Southside," Uncle Jay said.

Dirty finally lowered his weapon with his cold eyes. "If this all checks out, I will be back with your money. If not I'll be back with a body bag," Dirty said leaving and slamming his door.

Uncle Jay kicked his glass table over knowing he'd just put his life on the line. He had to get a location on his nephew so he could hand him over so he could get that check.,

"Daddy you, okay?" Redhead said, coming out from the backroom naked.

"Bitch get the fuck outta my face. Better yet get the fuck out you dead weight," he said grabbing her hair and tossing her out of his crib, naked.

She screamed and cried as Carolina laughed as she came out from the back.

Romell Tukes

Chapter 22

Olympia Field, IL: Weeks Later

Malik followed Face downstairs of his 14,928 square feet mansion in the rich, gated community where mostly rappers, NBA players, lawyers, judges, and drug lords lived. The downstairs looked like his own home with a game room, gym room, indoor basketball full court, and a movie theater. Face lived here for two years now only because people knew about this location for his safety and he stayed here without security because he had a state-of-the-art security system.

"You play ball?" Face asked, walking inside the double doors leading onto the basketball court with its shiny floor, bleachers, and two hops with a new fresh net.

"Of course," Malik said as Face passed him a ball.

They shot around for a while. When Malik received a call from Face setting up a meeting, he was gassed especially when he invited him to his open house that Simone didn't even know about.

"The cook should be done with the halal meal soon. I'm Muslim so I only eat hala, I hope you're cool with that youngin," Face said shooting the ball in the net.

"Perfect."

"I see you handle your business well," Face said.

"I follow the law of the streets."

"As you should, that's how you gain honor and respect, but let's talk business. How much weight you trying to cop and where do you plan on moving it? Because as you know mostly every section in the city is controlled by a gang," Face said sitting down on the gym bleachers.

"Depending on the price I want ten birds or fifteen keys," Malik said with a laugh.

"I don't know if anyone told you, but I sell weight, not feathers, kid. How much money do you have?" Face asked.

"Two-hundred-K and I have a crew in Chicago Heights who'll be coping the weight from me plus my personal clients," he replied.

Face was in deep thought. "Look I don't deal with chump change, but I like you and you're taking good care of Simone. So, I'ma do this for you. I'll give you eight bricks of some good coke. I sell the keys at twenty-K a piece, so I'll give you forty keys on the arm and thirty keys off the strength to get on your feet," Face said.

Malik was shocked at the numbers, he thought he was dreaming. He never knew Face was playing with that type of weight. Face had a crazy cartel plug for years so he controlled a pipeline throughout the Midwest.

"I'm wit' that I appreciate this."

"Respect, little homie, all I ask for is loyalty. The streets ain't the same no more."

"Facts, bro, everything is golden on my side."

"Good, but I want you to stay safe. I hear they've got some dangerous niggas called Chi'Raq something killer or Gangstas out there robbing niggas blind, so move cautious," Face said seriously.

Malik had on his poker face nodding his head. Malik and Face played a game of one on one and to his surprise face won by six points.

Southside, Chi-Town

Detective Rodriguez drove through the mean, dangerous streets watching gang bangers sell drugs on corners, hand to hand sells, dice games, fiends shooting up dope in alleys, hookers racing up and down the streets known as nightwalkers. Rodriguez saw a couple of hookers looking for a date, so he pulled over to the curb in his Benz E Class that he used as a work car. Most of the field scars were from drug busts and big raiders of kingpins in the city leading to their cars being impounded. Rodriguez saw a pretty little white woman in a black, tight, dress with heels showing some skin, legs, titties, and a nice ass.

"Hey, papi, you looking for a night in heaven?" Carolina leaned into his window flashing her breasts.

"How much?"

"one-hundred an hour and fifty for oral. I can make you come in two minutes if not you get a refund."

"Get in," he said.

She opened the doors and climbed inside then he raced off. When they were a block away Carolina took a deep breath.

"What you got for me?" Rodriguez asked his co-worker officer Bonds a.k.a Carolina she was new on the task force that they called the Hooker Ring due to the mysterious rape and death of their fellow officer who went undercover as a hooker to bust Uncle Jay but turned up rape and shot fifteen times in a dumpster last year.

"As far as Jay he's been going crazy over his nephew. I believe he paid him some money, it's all he talks about. I've been getting very close," she said putting on lipstick.

She hated going undercover, but the good thing is she really didn't sell pussy. Her coworkers would act like men trying to buy pussy and they would get her and pay her with marked money to bring back to Jay.

"Did he mention anything about Amanda's murder?" Rodriguez asked, as he stopped at a red light.

"He never talks about his old workers," she replied.

"Shit—okay, continue the good work."

"I will, but I think his nephew is in big trouble and his Chi'Raq Gangsta crew," she said.

Rodriquez pulled over pushing on the brakes hard. "What you just say?"

"His nephew Boss is with a crew called the Chi'Raq Gangstas. I think he trying to set his own nephew up."

"Tell me everything you know about them," he said.

He became excited to hear what she had to say. He'd been having sleepless nights since the body of Lil Rico was found on his front lawn. She told him everything she heard was known about Boss and the Chi'Raq Gangstas which wasn't a lot, but enough to start his investigation.

Southside

Boss walked out of a small fruit store early in the morning with two bags full of fruit for Rosie and himself because they'd chosen to start eating healthy. He saw a familiar face walking his way in a long t-shirt and dirty jeans.

"Boss, oh my God! I really need to speak to you," the redhead chick said.

Boss continued toward his car. Not one of them stopped to even talk to fiends or hoes.

"What because I see you going to follow me?" he said since she was on his heels.

"Your Uncle sold you out to a guy named Dirty whose sister was killed, and Jay gave you up for the money the man put on your head."

"What was the sister's name?" he said, testing her.

"Shay or Shayla, I forgot," when she said that Boss knew she was being one hundred.

"Why are you telling me this? Ain't you his main hoe or some shit?"

"Not anymore that bastard kicked me out the same day I over-heard him giving you up weeks ago," she said honestly.

"Thank you." He pulled out a wad of money and handed her 3K.

"I didn't do it for the money."

"I know but take that room at the Red Inn hotel. Take my number and get clean. You don't have to sell yourself anymore. I have a job for you, I'll be in touch with you in a week or so, love," he said.

She cried, he gave her his number and pulled off, getting ready to call Malik to tell him the news but he saw a text from him saying meet him at the park on Washington Street at 10:30 tonight.

Washington Park: Later

Boss pulled up under a streetlight in the dark park where people would come out to throw cookouts and fish in the lake near the play-ground area. Boss wore a black Gucci top and bottoms with a pair of black Timbs. Today was his birthday twenty-second birthday. He spent the day with wifey, they cooked and enjoyed each other's company, but Boss was focused on a bag. The money he had from Lil Moe was invested for Rosie to start her hair salon and for the next time, they were almost back to rock bottom. He couldn't wait to tell Malik what type of shit his Uncle was on. He walked toward the lake area with a bottle of Patron in his hand, looking into the bright star, sitting in their positions near the half-moon.

"You get a closer look any second at the stars," a deep voice said behind him.

He felt cold steel pressed to his temple as he calmly took another sip of liquor out of the bottle.

"Do you Gangsta."

"I will, Lord, and your little crew's next. I've been tailing your punk ass for weeks," Dirty said in Boss' ear.

Boss was feeling as if he was being followed lately by a blue BMW M2 Coupe but he brushed it to the side and regretted it.

"Did you think you were gonna get away with killing my sister?"

"Well, yeah, I did if it wasn't for my uncle," Boss said.

Dirty slapped him in his head with a silk pistol. "Malik's next, I can't wait. I got a special surprise for him," Dirty said grinning and about to pull the trigger.

"I love surprises," Malik said walking up behind Dirty blowing his brains out. *Boom! Boom!* Boss looked back surprised to see Malik standing there. "Come on let's toss his body in the lake," Malik said.

They dragged Dirty's heavy body over the wet grass until they made it to a small wooden deck. Dirty's body dropped in the water and sunk to the bottom within seconds and they walked off.

"I heard he was looking for us a few days ago. So, I followed him to his BM's crib on the West Side. I knew he was on to you when I saw him go visit your uncle. So, I called you today so you could bring him out here why I hide in the bushes the whole time. I knew he was going to drill your shit tonight, perfect setting out here dark, quiet, and private," Malik said as he walked into the lot where Boss and Dirty's car was parked.

Malik parked on the other side of the park.

"Smart and good looks."

"Happy G Day let's go holler at Animal he's waiting on you in the car. We got some bottles of Hennessy." Malik climbed in Boss' car.

They went to meet Animal across the park. They spent the night outside drinking and talking about Face and the keys he was about to receive tomorrow. The crew knew Face would be there to break through where they wouldn't ever have to rob anymore because it was starting to become a full-time job.

Chapter 23

Boss was eating dinner with his mom, something he rarely did these days because he was so busy. The past couple of weeks he'd been on a new mission with Malik since Face gave him all the bricks, he had a couple of niggas out of town hustling, so he'd been making a lot of business trips with Animal.

"I'm still mad you didn't invite me or your brother to your wedding. I'm upset about that," Janella said as she sat across from him looking beautiful with glowing skin and freshly done dreads in a ponytail.

"I'm sorry it was spur of the moment in Vegas," he said looking at her amazing baked chicken.

"Vegas, huh, you working now?"

"No."

"Rosie."

"No, I made her quit."

"What type of ring did you give her?"

"A Cartier ring, with a platinum setting and nineteen diamonds on each side and four baguettes."

"Woo," she said as she stopped eating. "You selling drugs?" she asked looking into his eyes.

"I just started doing that mom, I was doing something else before that," he said honestly, seeing the disappointed look on her face.

"You kids' just don't get it. The white man brought drugs into the states to corrupt our people and enslave us. You're giving them an easy way out to destroy our culture. You're a smart, handsome, young man. You have a way out, don't let them box you in—excuse me," she said leaving and going to her room.

"Mom, I love you," he said as she stopped.

"You can't love someone until you love yourself. Go see your father," she said hurting to see her oldest son be the victim.

Boss knew his mom disliked the use and selling of drugs. It was her pet peeve, besides rats and liars. Boss knew he had to make a long-term plan because he didn't want to be like his father who was sitting in prison for life.

Days Later: Hazelton USP, West Virginia

Boss was in the prison visiting room dressed in a Givenchy outfit with a Cartier watch. It was a small birthday gift he'd bought himself a couple of weeks ago. Animal was outside sleeping in the car while he paid his dad a visit.

Boss was out in Virginia for two days dropping off keys to his man Lace who was a GD from Chicago but was getting money in Bad News, Virginia.

The crew was getting so much drug money they didn't have to rob anymore. It was all they thought about during their alone time. When he saw his pops walk out with his gangsta bop, he laughed.

"Son, good to see you," Ty Stone said embracing his son.

"How are you looking younger every time I pull up?" Boss said.

His dad checked out his watch and gear. "That must be that designer shit I be hearing young men argue about all day," his pops said, looking at the big Givenchy sign across his black shirt in big bold letters.

"Yeah."

"That's nice, thanks for the money, but that's a lot of money. You could've opened a business with that ten gees."

"I'm focused on a business as we speak for my girl. She's about to open a nail soon and I'm trying real estate and opening a small car lot once I get my licenses."

"Good," Ty Stone said, smiling

"I'm on it just got a lot going on in them streets," he said.

His pops frowned. He knew his son was in the field, but he hoped he was smart enough to get out before sugar turned into shit. "You trust the men around you?" Ty stared into his son's eyes without blinking.

"Some, pops why you ask?"

"Let me tell you a story about before I got in the game. I had two best friends I grew up with since the sandbox. When I got my first six-pack I divided it into three so they could eat. When they caught little cases and had to do stints in the Cook County Jail, I held them down, looked out for their girls and kids so they would want for nothing. When I bust down, I divided my profit into three. I treated these niggas like brothers, they had keys to all my stash houses and numbers to my safes. I woulda did anything for them, I even killed for them, because niggas would rob them. They were too scared to do anything so since they were with me, I would spoil them just to make a statement—" he said, pausing.

You was loyal, pops?"

"Huh, loyal? Let me tell you something about loyal—being loyal got me a life sentence, taking me away from you, your mom, and my life. When I got locked up, I didn't receive a letter, a visit, no pics, damn sure no money from neither one of them, but I'll tell you what they did though. They took all my money a couple of millions and a couple of tens of dope and most likely busted it down the middle, but it's not the part that hurt me the worst," his pops said getting real emotion, Boss shook his head hoping his crew was different. "When I went to trial, these two niggas sold me to the feds telling them shit that didn't even have to do with the case. Telling lies and smiling in my face, they even winked a couple of times while laughing," Ty Stone explained with a serious look. "That's where my loyalty got me in here. So, because of who you're loyal to and because you may never know you were until it's too late."

"Facts, but who were the two dudes. They still out there?" Boss asked.

"Yes, that's the sad part, one of them was a guy named, Premium. He's a deacon in church now and the other was my brother, Jay"

"Uncle, Jay?" Boss said, shocked.

"Yep, he's the one who winked at me from the stand. But let's talk about something else. You're a married man now, I'm proud of you."

"Thank you, I'm happy and she's perfect."

"Good, good—they're about to end visits. Come back when you get time and stay focused. Trust no one not even me," his pops said embracing him.

Boss thought about the meaning behind his words.

Southside, Chi-Town

"You did good tonight, baby girl," Uncle Jay said, entering his building and counting the money Carolina gave him at Popeyes from a long night of tricking or so he thought.

"Thank you, daddy, I'm tired it's two a.m. I just want to sleep," Carolina stated in the building elevator.

"Sure, I got to go pick up two new hoes. I want you to train them. They're both runaways and on drugs so they're easy. One is sixteen and the other just turned seventeen-years-old, both are legal to me," Uncle Jay said in a careless tone.

She looked at him in disgust. Inside the dark apartment, which was dirty with an odor as always, he turned on the lights.

"Ohhh, shittt—" Uncle Jay said, seeing a young nigga who looked no older than fourteen-years-old pointing a Tech-9 machine gun at them.

Carolina went into panic mood. She had a work gun in her purse, but her chances of getting to it without being shot was thin so she tried to calm down.

"Jay, we need to talk. Word is you're the man connected to the Chi'Raq Gangstas and someone gotta pay for my brother's death," the young man said now walking toward them.

"You made a mistake, young blood. They call me, Willie," Uncle Jay said, he saw a tattoo of a snake covering his whole neck.

The kid laughed. "Okay, Willie!

Tat! Tat! Tat! Tat! Tat!

Bullets entered Carolina's skull and she fell on the wall slowly, leaving a bloody trail on the white wall as her body dropped to the floor in a sitting position on the wall with her hand on her purse.

"You got more, Willie jokes or you want to tell me who killed my brother, Lil Moe?"

136

"Canon," he said in fear, never seeing the killer's face until now. He'd heard stories of the young nigga's work and heard of his body count. "I know who they are but I know nothing about what happened to your brother. I Never heard of him but I can help you get the Chi'Raq Gangstas. One of them nigga's go by the name, Boss. He used to trick big on her," Uncle Jay said pointing at Carolina's dead body silently praying he wasn't next.

"Where he be at, Joe?"

"I don't know where he been lately, but he got a crew with him on Viceland. There's a kid named Malik and I don't know the other one's name."

"A'ight, I'll be back, Joe." Canon patted him on the back before leaving.

Canon was from West Chicago he was a snake, gang member, and a snake in real life. He was responsible for some of the most brutal murders on this side of town. He is dark with good, wavy hair, and a babyface just like Lil Moe at age twenty-eight. He was Freddy-V and Jasmine in one, he only came outside when it was dark.

Canon had all he needed which was the names of his brother's accusers. He could taste the blood on the tip of his tongue as he exited the back of the building knowing it was only a matter of time now.

Romell Tukes

Chapter 24

L-Town, Westside

Premium was his old name now he went by the name of Deco Bet-
tiuna, an active member of the West Holy Church across the street
from a car wash in the hood. Growing up Premium was raised on
the Southside in a Black Stone hood which he was a member of at
one point in his life. He grew up in poverty, his father was killed in
the tech army. His mother was a dope fiend, so he turned to the
streets like most did in that type of situation.

Ty and Jay were his best friend since he was five-years-old.
They were like brothers to him. When he went to school with holes
in his shoes Ty would give him his shoe and wear his back home.
When Ty started to get money that's when Premium saw another
side of life, the hustle, and the riches unaware of the tribulations.
Shit was great for the crew back then until Ty got arrested by the
feds.

Premium was sick because not only was his best friend in the
feds facing the death penalty but Premium had no money or drugs.
Ty's life was on the line and with a new child on the way in days
after Ty's arrest, he had to do something. One night he got up with
Jay and he told Premium about an idea to go get all of Ty's money
and drugs out of his stash spots just to keep the police from getting
it.

When he suggested that they should go speak to Ty about it
first, Jay went crazy on him and asked him how he was going to buy
diapers for his son and pay his bills. Premium knew he was right,
so he tagged along and that night they got them another load and
split it 60/40 because Jay said it was his idea.

The money and drugs lasted for about two years of good living
then after that, he hit rock bottom as well as Jay who sniffed most
of his shit. Premium's baby mother was the daughter of a pastor, so
she dragged him to church daily and one day he found the light and
never turned back.

Premium had just left the church. He always stayed late to make sure everything was in order and clean for the next day. His wife, Barber was his backbone. They lived a happy, faithful life submitting their time and life to the Lord. Premium walked into an empty parking lot in his Dior for men suit to his Cadillac truck taking in the cool night air. Once inside his car, he said a quick prayer as he did every time he got in the car. When he felt the gun to the back of his head he didn't move.

"You're going to need more than a prayer to get you out of this one," Boss said from the backseat.

Hours ago, he sneaked into his unlocked car and waited for him to come out. Premium had been on his mind since he visited his pops.

"I fear the Lord, not man."

"So, that's why you snitched on my pops and double-crossed him?" When Boss said this the man became silent and tears filled his eyes.

He thought about what he did but Jay got inside his head. Jay told him if they didn't take the stand then Ty Stone would, sure enough, kill them for what they did.

"I was young, and I made a mistake, but the Lord forgave me," Premium said

"The Lord did but the streets and my father didn't. You made my life hard. That's the thing with you snakes and rats, you only care about yourself. What about the families and children of the people y'all take the stands on?" Boss said speaking for all the niggas who experienced a lack of fatherhood because a rat took their father away from them. "In life, we make choices that we will face one day. I've been waiting for this day."

"Me too—"

Boom! Boom! Boom!

Boss didn't stop until the 9mm Glock was empty then he hopped out with a Valentino black hoodie and ran off.

Club New Secrets

The club was popping tonight bottles were being delivered to six VIP sections in the packed club. The DJ played the hottest sounds, females and niggas danced on the floor enjoying the vibes. Tonight was Lil' BD's birthday. He was in the VIP with five of his guys drinking and smoking.

"How does it feel to be twenty?" Hitler asked with a deep slur in his voice, from the Remy he'd been drinking all night.

"It feels the same, I wish Loso, Chubby, JT AD, and Beast was alive to enjoy this shit," Lil' BD said, dipped out in designer shit with a Celina outfit and Christian Louboutins on his feet. He was clean tonight.

Since being shot months ago he was laying low trying to chase a bag with Hitler. They had a plug on the team and molly so they had Buff City on lock with the help of the guys.

Lil' BD saw someone else enjoying their B-day party as a bottle with sparkles headed toward a VIP full of bad bitches. When Lil' BD saw the chick in the red Chanel dress with her hair down, he thought she was foreign until he got a closer look.

"Yo' we sliding over there," Lil' BD told the guys.

"Jenny—" Lil' BD said looking past six of her loud, home girls lining up to a Troy Lanes song blurring through the club.

"BD, oh my god. Hey, that was you over there," Jenny said brushing past her girls to hug him.

Hitler said damn a little too late.

"Come join us, it's my birthday," she said remembering that it was his too, she'd forgotten that they had the same birthday.

"It's mine too but happy B-day," he said.

She told him the same thing as her legs hung out of the side slit of her dress.

"You should keep your eyes in place where they can be controlled," she said smiling as Hitler looked over toward them to see what they were talking about.

Because he knew his boy and she had long gone, she had gone to. She was the baddest piece in the club.

"You should watch what you say if you can't back it up." He sat back drinking a bottle of Henny that had just arrived. She took the bottle from his lips and grabbed his hand and her purse.

"Y'all get him home safe," she said leaving with Lil' BD

"Bitch where you going?" her friend said.

"BD, it's like that?" Hitler said watching his bro' bounce as he looked back at the slim redbone he was talking to.

"So, we cute too?"

"Boy, please in your dreams. You still got baby teeth and wearing American Eagle jeans, acting like they Balmain," the chick said.

The whole VIP laughed until Hitler slapped the shit out of her before leaving as his guys stayed and macked on the bitches who didn't care or the redbone bitch.

"Ooohhh—Jenny," moaned as Lil BD admired her cocoa, brown-skinned with his tongue licking and sucking her hard nipples making his way down her naked body in her bed.

Lil' BD held her tone fit body, when he saw the perfect plumbed, clit sticking out between her intact pussy lips he flicked his long tongue around her clit slowly something he had dreamed of doing for years.

"Shit, nigggaaaa, umm!" she yelled as he increased his speed while placing two fingers into her wet tightness.

Her body quivered and squirmed in ecstasy to the motion of his tongue as she nutted on his tongue and finger.

"Justin, oh my goddd—" she said, shaking from his blessing he just gave her. "You're so nasty," she said as he licked her creamy tasty cum.

"You ready?" he said, climbing between her "Hold on. You want me to use a condom?" he asked because he didn't have one and he was hoping she did.

"I'm on the pill nigga and I trust you. Now come on, you're talking too much. You're killing my vibe."

When the head of his dick entered her, she jerked as his pussy muscles tightened like a lock because he was so big, she had no clue he was 12 ½ inches.

142

"Whattt, fuck nigga! You African go slow with that shit," she said as he pushed in and out.

He felt the heat of her body as she closed her eyes. Minutes later, her pussy was a perfect fit for his dick, and he drove his shaft deep in her.

"Uggghhhhh," she cried out as he hit her G-Spot with every stroke banging out her guts until they both climaxed.

She had to take a five-minute break. She had no clue Lil' BD was spanking a mandingo. Otherwise, she would have known that and she would have never invited him into her VIP.

Jenny took him from the back as she came twice on the dick. Then she did it sideways and in the air but he didn't get that treatment the first night, two hours later they were both snoring.

Romell Tukes

Chapter 25

100 Huella ST, Police Station

Detective Rodriguez sat in his office staring at the headline of the Chicago paper which read, *Undercover Officer Found Dead in Dumpster Again!* Rodriguez had a lot of heat on him due to the murder of Carolina a.k.a Officer Bands because he never got the investigation approval by the higher-ups so he'd been in deep shit.

This was the same thing that happened to Amanda. Her body was found in a dumpster alley. Not to mention he was having an affair with Amanda. She was a sexy, snow bunny fresh out of college. Everything in his life felt as if it was going downhill his job, his marriage, and even his semen count, due to stress and the lack-of-sex.

Rodriguez put out an APB on Uncle Jay just to question him about Carolina's murder because, at this point, he was at a dead end. There were no type of DNA clues or trails left at the scene, so he had nothing to go off which made his job so much harder. Then he thought about the Chi'Raq Gangstas. Could they be responsible for this? Was it, Uncle Jay? Did he find out she was a UC? Was it an angry client trying to force her to have sex and she rejected which lead to her death?

Rodriguez was trying to put everything together but first, he needed the key player Jay.

Buff City

Lil' BD and Hitler sat in his Cadillac passing each other the blunt filled with Sour Diesel and Kush mixed watching the block as BD sold molly and lean like clockwork. The block became a hotspot for lean and Molly. They were seeing 5K a day on the regular.

"Did you holler at the plug for more molly? We got like two keys left," Hitler said taking deep pulls from the blunt rolled up in backwood as it burned slowly.

"I'ma hit him tonight, bro. I wish Loso was here all would be straight."

"Facts, bro," Hitler added as the block darkened and niggas served niggas in alleys.

"You been hearing about them niggas out here sticking up all the big dawgs?" Lil' BD asked.

"Hell yeah, them niggas drilling shit, bro. I heard it's like ten of them niggas. They call themselves Chi'Raq Gangstas are GGs," Hitler said, he'd been hearing them niggas names heavy in streets lately, but nobody really knew who they were.

"As long as they don't come over here with that shit, we good but they probably killed Loso on the real."

"If they did, they got a big surprise coming," Hitler said, thinking of Loso who gave him his first pack after putting in some work for him.

"Facts, bro, anybody can get it for the big homie. But what you do after the club on my G-Day?"

"Mann—I had to slap fire out of that redbone bitch that tried to play me, Joe. You know I'm not an anything nigga," Hitler said.

Lil' BD laughed because Jenny told him what her friend called and said the next morning. She wanted to press charges, but she begged her not to.

"I heard, you a wild nigga."

"Fuck all that. What's up with you and that Indian and black chick, bro? She's fire, Joe, I've seen her before I just don't remember where."

'Nigga she's lived on the block forever she drives the Infiniti Q60 with the rims and tints."

"Oh, yeah, I remember her."

"Yeah, shawty, in college, got her own crib and she got a bag. I've known her forever, bro. We getting deep, she wants me to move in but mom not having it at least until she meets her," Lil' BD said. "That's a good look, bro. She's exotic and out of your league. You better hold on to that, bro, because the block hoes is washed up," Hitler said.

They chilled for thirty minutes then went to Hitler's hood to chill with the 4s.

Downtown, Chi-Town

Animal was in his Mercedes with Chole, who looked like a snack in her Off-White, yellow, and black dress with her strap on heels. To match her fly he rocked a white Salvatore Ferragamo outfit with a pair of white Dunhill shoes that went nice with his new Rolex Daytona 18K white gold, strap leather watch worth 30,000 at retail but luckily he got it for 20K.

"Where are you taking me?" Chole flashed her million-dollar smile, she looked stunning tonight with her Ladies Raget Tanagra watch and her GOA certified round brilliant diamond studs in 1.57 carats, H-color, VSI alarit, and 1.55 carats G odor VS2 worth 30,000.

"La DeVilla it's a French restaurant," he said.

She smiled, surprised he even knew about five-star restaurants. "Impressed."

"Then I got an art show lineup for us a little something you didn't know about me."

"I didn't," she said as they pulled into the large parking area.

Animal knew tonight he would hook her because he was showing her that he wasn't only an official gangsta but he also had class and knew had to switch it up when needed. Animal hopped out and went to her side of the car and a black Camaro with tints crept up on him with the window down just as he opened the car door for Chole.

When he saw the pole of the AK-47 he pulled out his Glock 27 with the 30-round clip.

"Get in the car!" he yelled, shoving her back inside the car as two shots entered his stomach ripping his abdominal muscles apart.

Bloc! Bloc! Bloc! Bloc!

Tat! Tat! Tat! Tat!

Animal and the gunmen were in a gun barrel of a lifetime as Animal shot out his window almost taking off his head.

Canon's rifle got stuck as bullets filled his car, he had no choice but to drive away, Animal wasn't letting up. Canon saw blood on his new red shirt that used to be white, so he was somewhat up in the scoring field.

When the gunmen were gone, Chole saw him collapse on the car, she climbed out and drug him into the car, taking him to a hospital. There was a hospital blocks away but she knew better than to take him there so she drove across town where patients were shot every five minutes and where he wouldn't have to risk being questioned.

Chole saw his eyes were closing and she touch his leg trying to keep him awake

"Hold on, baby, be strong."

Olimpiafield, IL

Face was in his eight-car garage standing over stacks of money pooled in Mountains, nodding his head to his best friend and childhood friend B. Stone.

"You moved all the shit faster than I thought, bro. And your money count is on point. We gonna do a lot of good business," Face said smiling.

Malik just stood there as B. Stone sized him up with his natural mean boy facial expression,

"I appreciate it, I'ma handle my business always and the work is fire."

"I know but I'ma get with you in a day. This time I'ma double you up, so I'll be sending one-hundred and sixty keys," Face said nonchalantly.

Malik wanted to jump in the air, but he played it cool. "A'ight," Malik replied, walking toward his car.

Face called out to him. "This weekend come thru for Sunday dinner my wife will be back from Africa and bring Simone," he said.

"Got you, fam," he said, leaving as he watched B. Stone watching his every move.

Chapter 26

Lincoln Park: Weeks Later

The summertime weather starts to break as the windy city starts to turn into fall too quickly. It was close to eleven p.m. at night and the crew had just arrived at their meeting grounds all dropped out in designer clothes and jewelry.

Boss looked at the men he considered brothers proud to see them doing good and flossing because they all came from the dirt.

"Animal, I see you in that shit bag," Boss said laughing but happy he was good and back to being able to walk again.

When they went to visit him at his crib after he got out of the hospital, he explained everything that happened and how Chole saved his life.

Chole stayed at the hospital all night with him until she knew for a fact, he was good. She never once questioned him about what happened, she was just glad he made it.

Animal saw the gunman's face and he knew who he was, he was at Cook County Jail with him years ago and he was a live wire. Word was he took craft in his murders and his body count was all of theirs put together times ten.

"It was a good drill, he woulda had me good if I ain't see him creeping."

"That's Lil Moe's brother. I can't believe he's on to us so fast. I wonder who else?" Malik said.

"We'll find out, homie, but until then I got a lick for us."

"Who?" Animal almost sounded thirsty.

"My big bro, Shooter," Boss said, speaking of his big homie.

"A'ight, let me know when. When I'm done with all the keys, I'll pay Face and divide the rest with us. I had the guys take them sixty keys to VA last weekend and I'm almost done with the one-thousand so we're gonna be sitting nice real soon," Malik said.

"When we go holler at Face if he is moving like this, we need to get him before someone else does," Animal said.

Boss shook his head. *"What!"*

"Animal, this going to be the biggest lick. Be patient. I'm building trust with him. Me and wifey just had dinner with him, bro. This nigga knows my wifey and layout so we gotta move smart," Malik said.

"Take your time, bro. I'ma focus on Shooter while Animal focuses on Canon. Our name is out there now I just gotta move smarter, protect our lives, and the bag," Boss said and they all agreed.

Harvey, IL: Days Later

Shooter was the big homie of almost 150 GDs in Chicago's inner city and Besavilla where he lived and sold pounds of weed. He was the weed connect and gun connect, he used to supply Boss. Shooter was driving in his gray Chevrolet Corvette Stingray on his way to meet Boss to discuss business. He liked Boss because he was a young nigga about his money, he was also about his growth and development that's why he brought him home years ago.

At forty, Shooter was still in the streets ripping and running but he had to feed ten kids, and going back to prison or getting killed wasn't in his game plan. That's why he stopped selling dope and crack fifteen-years ago because his homies were receiving too much prison time for crack and dope.

He pulled into the back of a warehouse, where he told Boss to meet him, when he saw the white creamy Denali tuck he knew it was Boss even before he jumped out of the passenger side of the truck. Shooter couldn't see who was in the driver's seat because the truck had presidential tints in the front and back window going all around the truck.

"What's good, folk?" Shooter said when Boss climbed into his car.

"Ain't shit, homie. How you doing? What's up with the guys?" Boss asked, trying to make small talk, he could tell Shooter was a little nervous.

"That's your man with you?"

"Yeah, that's my little brother."

"Oh, okay. What's up? What you need to talk about?" Shooter said, looking at his phone as it rang.

"This—" Boss said.

Shooter looked at him to see a .50 Caliber pointed at his face and he got cold feet.

"Where the money and drugs?" Boss demanded.

"Come on we family. You gonna do me like this outta all niggas? I showed you love youngin," Shooter cried.

"Nigga shut your bitch ass up. Where the shit at before I get mad in this bitch?"

"It's in the van, inside the warehouse, everything is in duffle bags. Boss, how you gonna cross me like this?" Shooter said before Boss blew his brains out all over the car window and door panel.

Animal and Malik hopped out with a gas can and fire.

"Light this shit up, I'll be back," Boss said.

He dashed into the small warehouse which looked like a big garage. When he saw the van, he opened the back door to see over eight large duffle bags. Without checking them he just hopped in the driver's seat and exited the warehouse. When she pulled out he saw the Chevrolet Corvette in flames and black smoke clouds filled the air.

He followed the truck back to the city thinking about how he'd just backdoor his homie but Shooter was all for himself any way he really wasn't for the guys. Plus, how much he had Boss paying for a pound he should have robbed him, he thought as he drove on the expressway.

103 Luella, Pole station

Uncle Jay got arrested as he was coming out of a dope house coping a bundle of good grade Heroin from some Spanish cats on the Westside section of the town.

He was in the bullpen sick and angry that Detective Rodriguez and a special gang unit raided the crib. The other niggas in the bullpen had gun charges, drug charges, and old warrants.

"Jay Miller—" a cop said reading his name off a clipboard.

He made his way out of the bullpen hoping someone had bailed him out but he'd burned every bridge with anybody who gave him a chance.

The cop led Jay to a back room where he saw his arresting officer sitting with a fold in front of him.

"Sit," Rodriguez said staring at the fake ass Katt Williams pimp.

"I don't know none of the dudes on there that's wasn't my dope."

"It was in your pocket."

"Somebody planted it. You have to believe I'm innocent."

"So was OJ but that's not why you're here. I need answers now and my first question did you kill this woman?" Rodriguez opened the folder showing him a picture of Jay and Carolina on a block outside of Harald's Chicken on 87th Street.

"Hell nah, I ain't kill her, she was my main whore. She made me a lot of money."

"So, you'll be willing to take a lie, detector test, right?"

"Yes, sure, right now," Jay was serious. "Anytime," he said.

Rodriguez believed him somewhat. "So, what happened to her?"

"The Chi'Raq Gangstas killed her," Jay said.

Rodriguez's face lit up like a Christmas tree. He stood up and rushed into the next room across the hall to grab a recorder, this was his big promotion. These kids were heavy around the city. He had a feeling they had something to do with Carolina's death. "They must've known," he said to himself.

"Why did they kill officer Bands?"

"Officer Band, who the fuck is tha?" Jay asked, seriously unaware of the newspaper and news reports.

"Carolina."

"Oh, yeah, sorry."

"Malik and Boss found out she was police and killed her period. I saw it with my own eyes. I was hiding behind a truck as they caught her," Jay said sadly.

"How do you know their names?"

"I know everybody."
"Will you be able to tell this to a jury?"
"Won't be the first or last time."

Romell Tukes

Chapter 27

Miami International Airport

Boss, Malik, and Animal got off their flight in Miami. The crew chose to get away for a couple of days and celebrate their riches from Shooter's lick. There were 275 pounds of exotic weed in the van and a little over 300K in twenties and fifties. Plus, two bags of new assault rifles that ranged from ARs, Sks, AKs, MPs, and RPGs with lasers and scopes attached to them.

Boss found a buyer for his portion of the weed his homie from Bossiville who was a 4 corner hustler had a section on lock with the weed game. Since Shooter was dead it was on season, but niggas needed a new weed plug. Having an extra 170,000 apiece they all sold the weed wholesale. The crew was up again. Everybody was stacking money except Animal he was blowing money on cars and jewelry. Boss paid for Rosie's salon and his car lot since he'd recently received his dealer licenses.

"This must be us right here, bro," Malik said when they saw a pretty, brown-skinned, thick chick in shorts standing in front of a Lamborghini limo.

"Welcome to Miami," the woman said smiling.

"Thank you. I assume you're our personal driver for the weekend?" Boss said seeing that she had on a limo driver's outfit with shorts.

"Yes, that would be correct. Where would you like to go?" she asked.

Animal stared at her bulging pussy about to bust out of her work shorts.

"Shopping," Malik said, feeling the blazing Miami heat.

"Well, we got Collins Ave and the Dolphin Mall. I see you gentlemen like designer clothes?" she said, looking at Boss' Versace outfit made for the summer with thin light fabric.

"We want to go to both areas if that's cool with you," Boss said.

"Sure, get in," she said walking toward the driver giving them a full view of her brown ass cheeks hanging out of the bottom of her shorts.

"Damn," Animal said before climbing inside the limo that could fit twenty people in its black leather, heated seats. There were two installed minibars, fully stock, digital iPods installed in the walls, and climate control, and two big flatscreen TVs connected to the walls to watch movies.

This shit is dope, Joe," Malik said as the limo drove out of the airport lot blasting the City Girl's new song through the surround sound system throughout the limo.

This was their first time in Miami, and they regretted not coming sooner. As they rode through the city streets they saw palm trees, luxury cars, nice, white, sandy beaches, beautiful exotic women, and all types of restaurants and shopping stores some of which they'd never heard of.

"This is Collins Ave, I parked in the Fendi parking lot because as you see it's packed out here today," the woman said. Animal asked her name. "Pearls."

"I bet," Animal added, she looked at him in the rearview mirror shaking her head because muscle, head niggas was not her type by far.

When she parked, they all hopped and made their way down Collins Ave except for Animal who approached Pearls.

"I was wondering if you wanted to have dinner later, Pearls? If you're not busy," he said as she leaned on the driver's seat door.

"I'm sorry but I'm busy." She prepared to walk off.

"It's like that?"

"Yeah, I like what you like. I'm not a hot dog type bitch. I like Cherry Pie," she said, she noticed that he still looked confused. "Nigga, I'm gay," she said then finally walked off.

Animal felt dumb as he tried to catch up to the guys who were already in the Michael Kors store buying up shit.

After hitting the Louis Vuitton, Gucci, Prada, Balenciaga, Ralph Lauren, Valentino, and the Tom Ford stores they were ready to hit the mall.

Chi'Raq Gangstas

In the mall, they split up and went in different directions. Animal was in the jewelry store Tiffany & Co. Malik was in a hat store, and Boss was in a Foot Locker store, checking out the new arrivals of Jordan's.

"Excuse me, but me and my homegirls wanted to know where you was from?" a cute, slim Cuban chick said dressed in booty shorts with a low cut tank top and Chanel signs all over it.

"Chi'Raq," he said looking at her five friends, three were Spanish and two were black who all looked like models.

"Oh, you must be visiting, you by yourself?"

"Nah, my guys somewhere in here."

"Y'all got plans for tonight?" she asked blushing

"Nah, we staying at the season one joint."

"Damn, that shit like five-K a night."

"Facts," he said as if it was nothing.

"How about we come through?" she said.

"A'ight fuck it, pool party. Bring some weed and pills. I don't know nobody out here," he said pul

ling out a wad of money.

"I'm from Little Haven, so I know the right people. What's all this for?" she asked, realizing it was over two-thousand dollars.

"Pills and weed," he said and she stuffed it in her bra inside her small B cup holder.

"Take my number, 305-417-1819. Call me when you ready," she said.

He called her back seeing that all her girls had a pair of shoes they were about to purchase.

"Treat yourself and your girls." He gave her another 5K from his back pocket.

She looked at him with her green eyes and model-like face. "Wow, thanks," she said at a loss for words.

Later

"These bitches better not be ugly or I'm clowning you forever! And ain't you married?" Animal said in the kitchen eating Five Guys.

"They not for me, they for y'all, bro. Facts, I'm not a horny nigga," Boss said looking at Animal and Malik while the doorbell rang. "That's them." Boss walked to the door.

When he let the women inside, Animal's dick almost jumped out of his trunks, they all walked into the luxury pad in bikinis with ass and titties hanging everywhere.

"This shit is crazy," one of the women said looking around to see a pool in the center of the floor, a bar near the terrace, a 45-foot ceiling, colorful wallpaper, fancy designs, Italian furniture, a fireplace built into the wall, a tiki bar on the balcony, and a state of the art stereo system.

"Let's get the party started," Malik said, forgetting he had a wifey.

Everybody climbed into the pool with rolled up weed, Molly, and bottles of Ace of Spades was passed around for them to enjoy.

Boss stepped out on the balcony to get some fresh air and watched his guys turn up with the bitches in the pool. He saw the Cuban chick coming outside looking for him.

"Hey, why you out here handsome?" she asked trying her best to hide her liking for him.

"What's your name?" He asked, looking at her colorful eyes. He had to admit she was dime piece.

"Alexis but everybody calls me Lexus, Boss," she let him know she knew his name.

"I'm married, Lexus, I'm just here for the guys no, disrespect your beautiful."

"Thanks, I respect that, I'm just chilling. We can be friends. I just like to have a good time you know."

"Yeah."

"You're Hispanic?"

"Yes, proudly."

They kicked it for a while outside talking and laughing while Animal took two women to his room for a threesome because they were both with it and horny. Malik ended up falling asleep on the couch with the other women while Lexus and Boss talked all night. They had so much in common it was crazy. They were the same age, had the same likings, and taste. She told him she was in college at the University of Miami studying to be a doctor. When he saw her Bugatti keychain, he asked her what was that for? She showed him her all-white Bugatti outside. He was shocked, he had no clue she was balling. They clicked heavy as if they'd known each other forever they promised to keep in touch as friends.

Romell Tukes

Chapter 28

Downtown, Chi-Town

Boss walked into the lawyer's office connected to the Bank of America to speak to one of the best appeal lawyers in the state of Chicago. His trip to Miami was good, they hit up a couple of clubs with Lexus and her friends and they had a blast. Lexus was a sweetheart and one of the baddest women he'd ever seen but he was a married man and Rosie was his life.

"I'm here to see Mr. Richardson," Boss said to an older, white woman sitting in the lobby.

"Do you have an appointment, sir?"

"Yes, my name is, Mr. Johnson."

"Okay an eight o'clock appointment. He's in the room with the door open at the end of the hall."

"Thank you," he said then made his way down the hall toward the smell of strong cherry scent.

Boss saw a black man sitting at a large oakwood desk going through papers with his head down.

"Mr. Richardson?"

"Yesss, you must be my eight o'clock?" The overweight man with a salt and pepper beard said leaning back and checking out the young man's Chanel attire.

"My father is in federal prison, he's been looked up for twenty years now. I heard you were the best appeal lawyer in the city. My pops got a life sentence and from what he tells me his case has a lot of loopholes. I'm willing to pay whatever," Boss said.

Mr. Richardson sat quietly, thinking for a moment. "What's his name and what type of case does he have?"

"Tyrell Johnson, and I believe it's the Rico murder, drugs and more maybe, I don't really know."

"Okay, I'll look into it, kid. If I'm one-hundred percent sure that I can take it, I will contact you. If not I'll let you know. I'm not into taking any people's money knowing their loved ones don't have fighting chances. Now if you were hoping I would charge you, I'll take your smile all the way to the bank," he said laughing.

"Thanks," Boss said, then stood to leave, hoping he could get his father out.

Boss thought it was fucked up that the man would give a nigga a life sentence because people changed their lives eventually and everybody should be entitled to a second chance.

Southside, Chi-Town

Lil BD and Jenny sat in his car talking, he wanted his mom to get back home from grocery shopping so he could introduce her to Jenny. Lil' BD and Jenny were serious now, they were crazy for each other, he'd even moved in with her recently. Shit was at its best for Lil BD he was getting money and living his best life.

"You good?" Lil' BD asked Jenny who looked good in her Fendi sundress and hells.

"Yeah, I've never met a nigga's mom before. What if she don't like me and think I'm just one of your thots?"

"Nah, my mom not like that, and I never brought anyone home. Plus, I told her about you already so no worries, my mom's official," he said looking at a gray Ford Focus parked down the block with tints and someone slumped in the driver's seat watching his mom's building.

Lil BD had seen this car parked in the same spot for two days, now he had a bad feeling about it.

Within seconds Janelle pulled up and hopped out with shopping bags.

"That's your mom?" Jenny said looking at the young-looking woman with long dreads, glowing skin, and a crazy body, her curves, and ass held up nicely in her jeans.

"Uh, yeah."

"No wonder where you got your looks from."

"I look more like my brother than anything," he said watching the Ford closely, he saw the driver load up a gun as his mom walked in her building.

"Your brother, you never told me you had a brother. And why you not helping your mom with the bags?" she said seeing his mom struggle with the shopping bags.

Lil BD pulled out his gun and cocked it when he saw the short, young nigga hop out of the car with a crazy look on his face as if he was zoned out on a mission.

"Pull the car down the block slowly and pick me up at the end of the block," he said.

She tried to say something but he was already gone.

Canon had been watching Janelle's building for two days waiting to see Boss but it was a no show and he was sick of waiting. So, he planned to pay his mom a visit. He had everything he needed to know about Boss thanks to street gossip. When he saw Janelle enter the building, he knew it was time. Even though it was early in the day which was rear for him, it was a quiet, windy day perfect for a murder.

Canon speeded across the street and walked up the small flight of stairs leading into the lobby. He had to find a way to get inside as he looked at the apartment numbers and buzzers. As soon as he was about to press a button a young nigga walked in with keys wearing a hoodie covering his face. Canon sensed something was off about him.

"Good looking, Joe, I forgot my key," Canon said.

The man opened the lobby door with his keys then spun around with a pistol trained between Canon's eyes

"Who sent you?"

"Nobody, I'm here to talk to Boss."

"Wrong answer."

Boom! Boom!

Lil' BD shot Canon between the eyes then ran down the block. He saw Jenny in his Cadillac at the stop sign waiting. When he hopped in, she drove off without saying a word as if nothing happened.

Tonight was the first night Chole and Animal chilled in private. They were at his apartment in his room which was large, with mink rugs, two king-size beds connected, a 52-inch TV, Prada sheets and curtains, a private walk-in bathroom, a walk-in closet, and mirrors on the ceilings.

"I know you not falling asleep on me big head," she said sitting up in bed with shorts and panties on with her legs wrapped around his watching a love movie.

"Hell no, I'd be a fool," he said as she laughed.

She enjoyed his company, they built a strong bond especially after she saved his life. When he went to Miami, she missed him every second. Animal had two bitches in the room with him in Miami thinking he was about to have his first threesome, but to his surprise the two bitch were a couple. They let him watch as they fucked each other but he wasn't allowed to touch, he was pissed but he didn't care it was an amazing sight.

"Your body is warm," she said rubbing on his bare chest as her hands traced down towards his shaft. This was the first time she ever touched him sexually with her soft hands and it was turning him on.

"Don't start no shit," he said

"What if I can't finish it." She kissed his lips as she grabbed his hard mandingo and made her way into his lap.

She took his thick dick into her warm mouth as she rubbed his balls while sucking the mushroom tip slowly.

She moaned, Chole wrapped her thick lips up and down at a rapidly fast speed as she savored his dick.

"I love this big dick. You like how I'm sucking your dick?" she moaned and slurped louder making a popping sound.

She positioned his dick getting it wetter. Chole took him down her throat stretching her jaw as his toes curled, she almost got his whole length down her windpipe.

"Uhmmmmm shit—" he cried trying to hold his head but pre-cum was all over her face and his sheets.

She didn't let up as she continued to force him down her throat as she gagged.

Animal stopped her and laid her down taking off her shirt to see her big, nice, breasts fall free as he took off her lace panties to see her pretty little pink pussy with her juices flowing out of her small pee hole.

He slowly entered her tight small womb. "Ooohhh damn, ssshhh—uhmm!" She covered her mouth to prevent screaming as his dick opened her up.

"Damn this shit good," he said going deeper as he thrust his hips into her throbbing pussy pushing her legs further back as she tried to help

"Punish this pussy!" she yelled, spreading her legs wider as her pussy gripped every inch.

He hit her bottom pussy walls with every stroke as they kissed and moaned then at the same time climaxed back to back.

She bent over showing him her big ass, he was at a loss for words. He entered her and she grinded hard on his dick fucking the shit out of his dick. She rolled her hips back, dropping low on his dick until he came and was now out of breath.

Animal ate her pussy and swallowed every drop of her sweet cum. They continued to fuck and suck until they both tapped out hours later. In the morning they fucked in the shower for two hours and went out for breakfast before he had to go to work. Animal was hooked; he'd never had pussy on her level, he felt as if she'd cast a spell on him through her pussy.

Romell Tukes

Chapter 29

Chicago Heights

Malik was parked in a Walgreens parking lot waiting on Face since he'd asked him to meet him here. The past couple of months the two of them built a strong bond and not to mention Malik was now moving bricks faster than a hoe selling pussy on Back Page. It was a cold, snowy day outside so he was dressed in a Tom Ford's suit and a mink coat worth 35,000 as he sat in his new Porsche Cayenne, Turbo truck album like he always did to put him in his zone. He saw a black Bentley with dark tints pull up. Malik hopped out waving his hand already knowing it was Face.

Once inside he saw Face on the phone dressed in his usually designer suit. Malik was admiring the creamy, soft, butter pecan seats, the mini bar, flatscreen TVs everywhere, climate control, heated recliner seats, and the digital keypad touch screen. There was no doubt in his mind the truck was made for royalty.

"What's going on youngin'? Nice Mink," Face said, hanging up his important phone call.

"It's my first," he replied because in Chi-Town if you had a real Mink you were somebody.

"Trust me you will see more ain't that right, Sheek?" Face yelled to his driver who was his young Shooter's sister's son.

"Facts." Sheek whipped the truck through the streets.

"Where we on our way to?"

"A flight on a private jet but the destination is a surprise. I think it's time," Face said smiling.

Malik hated surprises. "A'ight cool," he said leaning back enjoying the ride as Face kept looking over his shoulder and out of his back window.

"I think we have company. That Ford Explorer truck been following us since we left the Westside," Face stated looking behind two cars.

"You think it's police?" Malik asked wondering what the fuck was going on.

"Take them for a ride, Sheek," Face said smiling.

Sheek gunned the Bentley through the streets bending corners until they lost the truck which was easy.

"Yo', Sheek hit the carwash over there and go through the wash. I think we lost them," Face said as the Bentley went through the automatic car wash.

"That was close. What was that about?"

"Who knows but they will expose their hand sooner or later," Face said watching the long, blue soapy wipers clean the car in the dark drive-thru.

Bloc! Bloc! Bloc! Bloc! Bloc!

Sheek had flown to the other side of the car as Face raced for his pistol but the car door flew open and he was snatched out by two men with guns.

Malik hopped out and followed the two masked men, they forced Face into the Explorer truck then plugged a long needle into his neck taking all the fight out of Face before he blacked out.

"Y'all niggas almost blew it," Malik said from the backseat as he looked at Face's body curled on the floor.

"Nigga that's why we have your location on our phone scary nigga," Animal said driving.

Boss turned up the music blocking both of them out before they went back and forth all day like two bitches.

"Animal, we gotta take him to your crib," Boss said.

Animal almost pushed the brakes.

"Nigga, you wilding the fuck out. What about that building you just brought on Smith Street?" Animal said giving Boss a good idea.

"Perfect, but for our plan to go good someone has to be here we're going to do shifts. I got the mornings, Malik evenings, and Animal overnight," Boss stated.

"Why the fuck I get the graveyard shift?" Animal said pissed off.

"Because you have no life," Malik said laughing.

"Glad you think it's funny, bro," Animal said seriously driving back to Southside

Six Hours Later

Face woke up in a basement full of pipes, a staircase, two windows, carpets, a table, and a chair, cemented floors and walls, and a ton of loose wires.

"OG you been in the game too long to be lacking like this," Animal said as Face tried to see if he knew whether the face was fresh.

"Sorry about this Face, I'm most sorry but you a good dude but you know how it goes in Chi'Raq and if you was wondering whether Chi'Raq Gangstas," Malik said as Face silently cursed himself.

"Where is your stash at? And we want the motherload, Joe," Boss said.

"It's in my mansion, everything is in my panic room which is located in my walk-in closet in the master bedroom," Face said clearly as if he knew the question before he answered while looking at Malik and thinking about how he'd let a young nigga cross him. B. Stone was out of town in Atlanta trying to open a strip club and network.

"East," Animal said, seeing the double restraints he'd placed on Face's hands and ankles so he couldn't move if he tried.

"I'ma go because I know his mansion in and out, stay here. I'ma call y'all asap." Malik walked upstairs to complete mission one, but he knew missing two was going to be rougher.

Two Hours Later

Malik placed the last bag in the truck, he was sweating because this was his 12th trip back and forth. He had the truck seats down to make room for the drugs and money, there was so much he couldn't even add it tonight. Face had a secret panic room full of money and drugs. This was the crew's biggest lick all in one. They could really return now and focus on getting money at least that was his plan since he already had clients and work. When he made it back to the building Boss brought days ago he called the crew upstairs so they could help him bring the bags inside.

As soon as Malik opened the back truck the bags fell out of the trunk since it was so packed.

"Shit!" Boss said bringing the bags into the empty building, it was dark out and the area was a quiet, low-key neighborhood around the corner from the projects.

It took them 2 ½ hours to count the money on money machines. He had his car parked down the block. There were 2.3 million dollars in cash and 670 keys of coke in is house.

"Now mission two we bus that shit down later," Boss said walking down the wooden stairs into the basement to see Face lying on the floor calm.

"The money and drugs were recovered from the spot so everything is good," Boss said.

"Okay, hear no evil see no evil. Y'all will never see my face again," Face said hoping they'd cut him loose but the look they all had said differently.

"If I could I would, Face. There is only one moe thing we need before we can let you go free," Boss said.

"What's that?"

"Your connect," Animal added.

Face's eyes widen knowing these young punks were crazy and out of their league.

"That's not happening, you can just kill me. Plus, trust me you don't want to know who my plug is," he said seriously with a crazy look.

"Oh, you're gonna tell us, trust and believe," Malik said as he pulled out a blow torch and made his way over toward him, and placed the heat on his leg.

"Ahhhhhhhh!" Face yelled in pain as fire burned his flesh.

"Who is your plug?"

"Fuck you!"

Malik placed the torch on his right ear, burning it until tears fell from his eyes and his screams stopped him.

"How about now, Joe?" Malik said laughing. Face remained silent.

"We out, Malik, we'll be here in the morning, big boy. And don't kill him, just play nice," Boss told Animal as he started stepping in his face with his Timbs until Face passed out.

"Maybe," Animal said, pissed he had to babysit instead of sleeping in some good pussy.

Romell Tukes

Chapter 30

Hazelton USP Prison

Ty Stone came from the education building in his creased tanned uniform that inmates had to wear when leaving the unit except for inmates going to outdoor rec.

"Yo', Ty you got legal mail the C.O. put it in your cell," an inmate said watching sports center, sitting at a table with one of his wild homies. The three of them loved to jerk off to the female C.O. behind the cell door as they did their rounds inmates call them gunners.

"Thank you." Ty went upstairs wondering what could it be because his appeals were all denied years ago. He had one left, a 2255 unless a miracle happened, and in prison that was rare.

Once in his cell, he saw the letter on his desk from a Richardson Law firm with his name on it. He started reading the letter and his heart started to race.

Dear Mr. Johnson,

I'm Mr. Richardson out of Chicago an appeal lawyer. I was asked to look over your case by your son to see if it had a fighting chance. After looking through all 3585 facts trial motions and 3500 material you have a lot of serious loopholes that will get you back in court. Your son paid the cost for my services so I'll be putting in your appeal soon and briefing you. If you have anything you will like to add send it to my address below.

Ty sat on his bed after 20 years in prison he never had any real hope until now. He couldn't believe his son did a stand-up thing like this. He made his way downstairs to call him to thank him as tears of joy and hope welled in his eyes.

Lil' BD and Jenny were chilling in the rib drinking, smoking, and fucking as they did most of the time when they weren't out chasing a bag.

"What we doing this weekend?" Jenny asked as they laid on the couch eating ice cream and watching *Killer Season* the movie. They only watched gangsta films like the *Godfather, Scarface, Dead Presidents,* and her favorite movie *Set It Off.*

"It's up to you but me and Hitler gotta go out town for a couple of hours. We got a new plug on the pills and mollies some rich white boys," he said.

"Oh, damn, I gotta study for my exams anyway. So, I'm home-bound. Plus, I'm on my period and I hate doing anything when it's that time of the month," she said playing with his dick getting him horny.

"You must be trying to run a red light then," he said as his dick continued to grow.

"Oh, fuck no I don't play them games. But I can help you, daddy," she said sitting up and diving on his lap. He pulled out his dick, she licked his tip with her tongue ring while jerking him off.

"You like that, huh?" she said deep throating him trying to take his whole pipe.

She made her way up and down, making slurping sounds as she picked up the speed giving him sloppy top, spit, and pre-cum flew everywhere. When he came, she swallowed every drop like a champ before going back to eating her ice cream.

"How about the back door?"

"Nigga, you lost your mind. My asshole is too tiny to be played with. You better find you one of them white girls down the streets," she said.

He couldn't help but laugh, Jenny was funny and crazy but real. He liked everything about her he could see himself spending the rest of his life with her and raising a family.

Westside 116th

B. Stone was in one of his trap houses, full of his shooters. Who would shoot for him at the drop of a dime. When he got back from out of town he went to check on Face to tell him about his trip since his phone we was dead or off which threw him off balance. Upon entering the mansion he saw the back doors leading into the back yard busted which alerted him.

B. Stone searched the mansion and no signs of Face, he remembered Face telling him he was about to take a flight with his young boy Malik somewhere. He called Malik to only get a voicemail. He knew something was fishy but when he went to Face's stash in his panic room that said it all. He knew then that he'd been robbed blind and most likely killed.

"B. Stone what if it was them Chi'Raq Gangsta niggas? I heard they be kidnapping all the niggas with a big bag. One of his soldiers told B. Stone and he knew it made sense, but he had no clue who they were, he'd just been hearing their names a lot in the streets lately.

"Find out who them niggas is all of them, but our main target is the nigga Malik the Vice Lord."

"I hate them Vice Lords!" one of the young Stones yelled who was down with the speed demands from the 150 block.

"I got fifty-K for them Chi'Raq Gangstas and one-hundred-K for whoever can bring me, Malik," B. Stone said before leaving the crib with his two bodyguards who was only seventeen-years-old with big guns ready to lay any nigga down.

K-Town, Westside

King Mike whipped the new white Cadillac Escalade truck through the snowy streets on his way to an autobody shop to meet Boss. King Mike was twenty-five-years old and rich. He was a plug and Rosie's brother. He was neck to neck with Face. They both had the city on lock but him mainly. He had a lot of rank because his father was the first Latin King member in Chicago but he was doing life in prison so he left the streets to his son.

King's plug was in Miami and had the best cake and dope at great prices which was how he showed love to his people. His best friend King Papi was the face of his drug trafficking; they had a few killers, workers, mules, and blocks all over the city. King Mike's main income was from New York; his homies in the Bronx had him coping 800-1000 keys at a time.

Romell Tukes

When he pulled into his shop he saw that it was busy as always, he saw Boss leaning on a red Land Rover in a peacoat. He liked Boss. He was a good kid and took good care of his sister because she never wanted for nothing and she was happy, so he was for her.

"What's up, King?" Boss embraced him as if they were best friends.

"Come inside we can chop it up," King Mike said as he made his way into the shop to see niggas fixing cars all over the place.

Inside his office, he closed the door and took off his Bugatti coat checking his big face Richard Miller watch.

"What's going on, bro? My sis' hit me and said you needed to get at me," King Mike said sitting down behind his small desk filled with papers.

"I need a new plug I was fucking with a dude name Face but he was taxing me and he just vanished."

"I thought you sold weed, why change lanes?"

"More money and my people go to VA and Maryland to work so we be moving close to five-hundred keys in two to three weeks," Boss said.

King Mike looked amazed. "Damn, so you was fucking with Face, huh? How come you didn't approach me?"

"My man knows him, and he was already doing business with him," Boss said.

King Mike nodded. "I heard he disappeared shit's real out here. Niggas ain't making it but I can fuck wit' you, bro. You're basically family and I know you're a standup nigga. How much you want to spend?"

"First shipment a mill."

"You holding like that, bro? I got you when you're ready."

"Now," Boss said as they discussed a pick-up and drop location and popped a bottle of Henny toasting to success.

176

Chapter 31

Southside, Chi-Town

Malik's mama and step dad Steven was in Wal-Mart shopping Center doing some shopping late night shopping was a perfect time because the stores were normally empty.

Sha Malik's sister's death kept his mom emotional and distant from her son because she knew he was in the streets and she lost her daughter because of his Karma. One day she knew God would give her the strength to forgive him but right now she just wanted him to stay far away.

"I forgot the cat food, baby," Steven said as Roxy stopped and looked at him because he knew how much she loved her two cats.

"You can't be serious, babe," Roxy said, not wanting to go back inside, pushing the cart full of bags.

"I am but I brought some the other day so we should be good until I step out again," he said walking toward there Chevy Malibu as shoppers walked past them on this dark windy night

"Did you pay the light bill?" Roxy asked stopping the shopping cart at the Malibu.

"Baby, you ask the dumbest questions but you gonna let a nigga get deep in them guts tonight," he said smacking her big ass.

"Maybe if you can get it up," she joked because he had a serious ED issue which she hated but when he was up it was on and popping.

"Mmm—okay, well maybe if your pussy didn't always smell like cat litter or the garbage truck on Thursday mornings we would have no problems," he said closing the trunk.

Her face was balled up, She definitely felt disrespected. "I know you ain't just go there nigga!" she yelled getting ghetto as she did at times.

"Man get your ass in the car," he said, seeing a man coming their way and not wanting civilians in their personal business.

Boc! Boc! Boc! Boc! Boc! Boc!

Steven and Roxy both laid on the ground blocking at their head and face and B. Stone walked off as if it wasn't him while civilians speed-walked to their cars wondering where the shots were coming from.

B. Stone breezed off in a Ford Taurus back to his hood with one phase of his mission complete. One of his soldiers received info on Malik's family mainly Steven who was fucking with his mom. So, when B. Stone received this he was more than delighted to put some pain in.

Every day he thought about Face's whereabouts if he was dead, alive, or in jail. But what he did find out was that he was at war with the Chi'Raq Gangstas which started to make sense to him. The other two names Boss and Animal were foreign to him, but he planned to do whatever he could to seek revenge for his friend's death or mysterious disappearance.

Hazelton USP, West VA: Months Later

Ty Stone was in his cell staring out his window shocked by the news he'd just heard from Mr. Richardson, his appeal lawyer. He told Ty the Supreme court granted his appeal so he would be given a court date soon to either be resentenced to lesser time or to be released. He couldn't believe this was happening never in 100 years would he have thought that he would get his life back. He saw a lot of niggas giving their time back but never did he think he would be next up. Ty had many nights crying and missing his loved ones. His life, his freedom being in prison made him value the little things in life like the trees, sidewalks, light poles, grass and even watching cars drive by something you would never see in prison because of the brick wall and fences.

Coming to prison as a young man he had to learn a lot because the rules were somewhat different from the streets but the two things that were the same were every man was for himself and you can't trust a soul.

He saw a lot of young niggas lose their lives in prison by accident. He saw niggas lose their lives over a blow with months left to go home. He saw a D.C. nigga get murdered over some stamps worth nothing. Seeing these things would make any nigga cold-hearted and cautious around others in the belly of the beast. There was no such thing as a friend because they mainly turned into enemies.

Ty read the letter he received days ago from his lawyer for the 100th time as he reflected on his conversation with his lawyer because it felt unreal. The prison was on a month lockdown because ten inmates stabbed each other badly over two pieces of K-2 and paper which the jails loved to smoke and trip off of. He even saw a nigga jump off the top tier face-first high off K-2.

One mistake could change a man's life forever. Ty wished he would've known the shit he knew now twenty years ago, if so, he wouldn't be here.

Southside, Chi-Town

The crew still had Face in the same location as they did months ago. They had no plans to let him go no time soon. Not until he gave up his connect. They tortured him every day until he was unconscious but he still didn't break. They knew whoever his plug was had to be someone special if he was willing to die in his honor.

Today Animal pulled a double shift because Malik went to his mom's graveyard to put fresh flowers on the tombstone as he did weekly. The murder of Malik's mom had Malik ready to wage war on the whole city.

Malik said he believed it was Face's people a nigga named B. Stone. When he approached Face about it he laughed in Malik's face hard. Malik beat the shit out of Face almost killing him. Boss and Animal had to snatch him off him, he was stomping his head into the ground.

Animal was in the basement asleep on the couch while Face was wide awake sharpening a chicken bone he'd been working on for three weeks now.

Face looked different with broken ribs, a broken jaw, broken eye socket, nose, missing thirteen teeth, a fucked up eye, and cuts all over his face. He quietly continued sharpening the thin needle-like sharp bone he stated cutting the sharp tool off his hand restraints.

After two hours of cutting, the hand restraints came off, so he focused on his ankle restraints but Animal's movement scared him and he played sleep. Animal checked on Face who looked sleep and went back to the couch and went to sleep snoozing.

Face went to work cutting his ankle restraints sweating as if his life depended on it which it did. Two and a half hours later he set himself free and almost cried with joy, he saw Animal on the other side of the basement sleep.

He was going to plunge the bone into Animal's neck but it was too short and there was no way he could outrun and wrestle with the large man so he weighed his choices and crept upstairs slowly not making a sound.

Once upstairs in the dark abandoned house, he saw a hoodie laying on the floor. He picked it up and put it over his bare chest. Luckily, he had on a pair of old sweatpants they placed on him when he first got here.

The coast was clear as he ran out of the building onto the dark block which looked like a nice neighborhood but it was unfamiliar turf to him, he put his hoodie on and walked down the block.

Face looked behind his shoulder as cars past him, when he made it to a block with young niggas chilling he asked to use one of their phones to call B. Stone who was happy to hear his voice at 1:00 in the morning.

***

Malik was driving down the block, making his way over to check on Animal. So, they could switch shifts he just wanted to pay his mom her weekly night visit. Simone told him that a detective name Rodriquez had questioned her about him the other day. He told her not to worry,

Inside the abandoned building he saw the front door was wide open which was weird because the crew only used the back to keep people out of their business. He closed the front door and made his way downstairs to hear Animal snoring loud. Malik went to check on Face seeing that he was gone, and his restraints were cut off and left on the floor in the corner.

"What the fuck? Animal!" he yelled.

Animal woke up grumpy because he didn't want to hear it, he had plans with Chole, earlier. "What?"

"Face's gone, bro. Come on," Malik said.

Animal hopped up shocked because the last time he checked he was asleep.

"Fuck—he was just here!" Animal shouted following Malik upstairs.

They drove around the whole neighborhood to come up with nothing. Malik told Animal he could've sworn he saw a nigga in a hoodie who looked like Face but it was too dark outside.

"We gotta call, Boss," Malik said driving his Porsche through the city.

"Boss, this nigga let Face get away, bro. We in deep shit" Malik paced the parking lot.

"Don't worry about Face, we got a bigger problem. A detective's been following me for a couple of weeks now. I gotta feeling my uncle who was putting us on them licks gave me up, but I did my research on this nigga," Boss said.

"Hold on, bro. Is his name Rodriguez?" Malik asked.

"Yeah, how you know?" Boss asked suspiciously.

"He pulled up on wifey asking about me."

"Damn, he on to us," Boss said, feeling as if shit was going downhill.

"Yeah, nigga, it's hot out here," Animal said.

"If he on to us then he on to *you*. So, we gotta do something soon. I have a plan but after this, we have to lay low," Boss instructed.

"We already have enough money and work. I'm not trying to get trapped off so I'm all in," Malik said.

"It's never enough money but least do it when you ready hit us, Joe," Animal said, looking at his new Audemars Piguet Royal Oak watch 18K rose gold on an alligator band to see it was 2:45 a.m.

"A'ight," Boss said, leaving stressed out.

Weeks Later

Detective Rodriguez got off work on his way home to his wife who was most likely asleep, so he made his way to his favorite bar in his work car to get a couple of drinks.

He'd been so busy at work focused on the Chi'Raq Gangstas case, trying to pin Carolina's body on Malik and trying to figure out who the other man was and what they were doing in the rundown abandoned building at all hours of the night.

He had to update his boss on his process every week so he could stay on the case and his chief saw something big in the case, he just wanted him to be safe because he could tell these youngsters were a different deadly breed.

Rodriguez went into the empty bar filled with less than twenty people and had a couple of drinks but by the time he was ready to leave he was pissy drunk from drinking whisky.

He stumbled outside the bar toward his crown Vic and fumbled for his key in his slacks while he started talking to himself.

"Run my life, fuck a marriage and a job, I'm a king!" Rodriquez yelled with a slur as he made it to his car barely able to stand up.

"What you say?" a voice said behind him.

"Mind your damn business that's the problem with you people today," Rodriguez said, not even looking back as he placed his key in his car door about to climb in.

Whack!

A golf club knocked Rodriguez cleanout and the aggressor picked his body up and tossed him over his broad shoulders then threw him in the trunk of a stolen Honda Accord filled with two other men known as the Chi'Raq Gangstas.

An Hour Later

The crew was on a boat sailing down the dark Chicago River with Rodriguez held at gunpoint by Animal and Malik while Boss whipped the boat.

"Why us?" Malik asked.

"You killed officer Bands," Rodriguez said

"Who?" Malik asked, confused.

"Carolina," he said getting Boss' attention

"Jay told you that?" Boss said Rodriguez stayed silent and that said it all. "That nigga set us up, my Uncle," Boss told his crew.

"So, you didn't kill Carolina?" Rodriguez asked feeling dumb, that he'd let a junkie like Jay outsmart him.

"If you would've known, would you have risked your own life for some false info?" Malik asked as Animal laughed.

Rodriguez wondered why Animal looked so familiar, but he couldn't put his finger on it and the knot on his head made it hard to think clearly.

"Y'all been the ones killing all the gang leaders and drug lords I guess, huh? And now I'm next?" he remarked, they were all quiet. "Look guys let me go and I can make this right. If not, they will bury you under the jail if anything happens to me. Save yourself this is not worth it," he said as everybody started to laugh.

"How long we got until we bring the boat back?" Boss asked Malik.

"My people said we can use it all day if needed. Shit, for five-K in this little shit it should be free. I didn't know you could drive a boat, bro," Malik said.

"Shit it's just like a car," Boss heard Animal say as he shook his head, looking at Rodriguez who laid on the floor now looking nervous because he was scared of oceans and he couldn't swim.

"It's time," Boss said.

They were two hours outside of Chicago in a town called Springfield. Animal and Malik grabbed Rodriguez trying to toss him into the deep shallow river as he put up a fight, screaming until his body finally dropped into the water.

Rodriguez couldn't swim and he flopped into the water yelling, "I can't swim!" He drowned to death seconds later.

Boss knew this was a perfect crime setting, a drunk man falling off a boat and drowning, was an everyday event.

"That's done. Now we lay low until this shit blows over," Boss said.

Malik and Animal agreed as the boat turned around headed in the direction it came from. It felt good killing a cop but none of them would say it.

Chapter 32

Downtown Chicago: Two Months Later

"Baby this will look nice in our new bathroom. What you think?" Simone asked Malik pointing at a marble two sink counter in Home Depot.

"Just say you want your own sink," he said kissing her shoulder.

"Boy, we're getting it so write it down so they can deliver it," she said walking towards the tile and roofing area.

Last week Malik brought her a two-story home in Robinson, Illinois in a middle-class area she was so happy because it was her dream, now she planned to work on having a baby and marriage.

Since the killing of Rodriguez, the crew hadn't seen each other; they all were laying low until the heat fanned down because Chi'Raq Gangstas was a household name. The news of Detective Rodriguez drowning hit the media hard, but they didn't see any foul play while investigating his death besides his blood alcohol level was at an all-time high.

The chief of police of Chicago thought differently when Rodriguez's body was washed up onto the shore days later. They search for his boat to see if he'd fallen off but came up with nothing.

The only thing possible was that someone had to bring him to the river and toss him into the water area he swam for hours just to drown which didn't make sense.

Malik had crews of workers selling drugs for him in Chicago Heights and the city, he was seeing major paper while Boss was in VA checking a bigger bag because the work was going for double out there. Nobody had a clue what Animal was doing with his money or drugs, but he was happy.

"I think we got enough shit for today but who is going to put all this shit in the house? I hope you're a handyman," Simone said as Malik looked at how fat and big her ass was getting.

"You know I'm a handyman. How about I show you better than I can tell?" he said gripping a handful of her big soft ass as a couple looked and shook her head.

"You need to stop, cause people looking at us like we're porn stars," she said, putting down her Louis Vuttion dress that was holding her ass and curves in place.

After paying for the pre-ordered shipments they requested to be delivered to their home, they left on to the next location which was a Costco up the hill of the shopping center.

When they stepped outside the early morning sun and heat hit them both. Malik saw two men sitting at the bus stop reading a newspaper but peeking at him. He also saw two black vans driving around the parking lot and two SUVs sitting to his far left with white men staring at him.

Malik was always smart about his surroundings and this was one of those times, his gut told him something was wrong.

"You remember the lawyer's number that I gave you a while back?" he said holding Simone's hand.

"Yeah, why?" she asked.

"Call him and I love you," he said as police came out of everywhere with guns drawn.

"Get down! Get down now!" 'They yelled coming from everywhere.

Malik got on his knees with hands in the air, they tackled him to the ground and placed cuffs on him, cop cars were now all over the parking lot. Simone stood there crying feeling as if it was a dream or a nightmare. She watched over forty police officers take him away.

East St. Louis, IL

Uncle finished with one of his drug treatment groups and as he walked downstairs to the cafeteria area to eat lunch with the rest of the drug addicts.

He'd been in a long-term rehab center for months now trying to kick his dope habit but his real reason for being here was to hide from his nephew Boss.

When he ratted him out to Rodriguez, he had no clue Boss would find a way to have Rodriguez killed. He had to get away quickly because if he knew Rodriguez was on to him, he knew Boss put two and two together and knew he snitched on him and his crew.

Uncle Jay didn't know Boss was this vicious, he reminded him of Iman Sa'id back in the day that dangerous muthafucker. Without a penny to his name or a hoe on his side, Jay was down bad, now he wasn't shit except an old junkie stuck in his ways. He grabbed a PB & J sandwich and went to have a seat in the corner to look out of the window as he did every day.

Yo' Jay what's up, player?" an old school pimp and ex dope fiend named Bob asked walking up to him with a cane. Bob's name used to be heavy in the pimp game.

"What's up, Bob?"

"Just checking on you. Oh, shit I forgot to give you this letter some kid pulled up in front of the building in a nice car and told Floyd to give this to you, Joe," Bob said handing him the letter before walking off.

Uncle Jay opened the envelope and pulled out the paper which only had two sentences.

Hey, Unc, I must say that was a brilliant scheme on me but double shame on you. Enjoy your vacation. Nephew!

Uncle's hands started to tremble with fear as he wondered how he'd found him here but now that was his last worry. He had to get the fuck out of there as fast as possible this second hi legs and feet were numb.

Downtown Chicago

Animal and Chole arrived at the private landing strip to see a nice private jet awaiting them. She parked her Maybach and climbed out in a purple Valentino dress with slits on both sides showing her legs and thighs

"Come on, baby," Chole told Animal as he got out in a Ford suit as if he was about to go on a business meeting but in reality, he didn't have a clue where she was taking him.

Animal had been laying low lately, focused on building something real with Chole but she was such a bossy woman. Life was great the only thing that was eating him alive was Malik's arrest on the news it said he was arrested for the murder of a female under-cover officer and his crew was being investigated for the murder of Detective Rodriguez.

When Animal heard the news, he started thinking that Malik would rat him out. So, when Chole came up with an idea to go a vacation he was more than ready.

"This is a nice jet," Animal said following her up the stairs to the luxury jet.

"Thanks," she said sitting down on the peanut butter seats flip-ping off her heels getting comfortable

"This yours?"

"Yeah," she said flatly plugging on her iPhone into the wall un-der the flatscreen TV in the outlet.

"Where are we going?" he asked as the flight was about to take off.

"It's a surprise but first I want to talk to you about building a strong relationship. I'm ready to take it to the next level," she said as she looked into his eyes.

"I feel the same beautiful," he said holding her hand as the jet glided through the sky.

"I know who you are, DeWayne."

"Of course, I told you everything," he said laughing.

"No—I know who you really are, Animal. You and your two friends are the Chi'Raq Gangstas and I'm very impressed with how you carried yourself," she said as his face turned thinking if she was the feds.

"Who are you?"

"I'm Chloe Rodriguez you recently killed my husband, Detec-tive Rodriguez. But you made it look like he drowned which was smart, but you could've done better," she stated looking at herself in the mirror.

"You married? Was this why our time together was very lim-ited?"

"My husband and I were on the rocks for years it was only a matter of time before I would've had him killed and receive his death insurance, but thanks to you it worked out perfect," she said and Animal was past confused.

"So, I was your pawn?"

"No, you just met me at the right time."

"So, you don't really own an industrial engineer company?" he asked as she laughed.

"Do I look like I do?"

"Wow—okay, I ain't tripping; I just wish you would've kept it real from the jump," he said sounding upset.

"I'm sorry it's just that I had a lot going on and I didn't want you to get caught up in my mess."

"I feel you, but you have no hard feelings that I killed your husband?" he asked seriously

"Hell nah, you did me a big favor and I'ma show my appreciation by sucking and fucking you this whole vacation," she said sexually.

"Oh, I can go for that."

"That's not all, it's only the half Animal there's some more important things."

"What?" He gave her a mean stare.

Cook County Jail

It had been six months since Malik got arrested for the murder of an undercover cop who was found in a dumpster, he was also facing charges on the Rodriguez killing. He had a paid lawyer on container, and he came to see him weekly to update him on the case. The lawyer informed him they didn't have any DNA on Carolina's body, no videos of him around the crime scene, or nothing that would be useful at trial.

Malik asked about the witness and his lawyer explained the witness was now MIA somewhere and that was all they had on him. The lawyer also told him they spoke and the main reason for his arrest was because they believed he had something to do with Rodriguez's murder a while back, but they wanted the Chi'Raq Gangstas.

When the police asked him about the Chi'Raq Gangstas he played dumb as if he'd never heard of them before, but they didn't believe him. Malik was on his way to the shower in his unit wearing shower slippers as inmates sat around the TVs yelling and watching LeBron James play against the Miami Heat which was a good game. There were seven Vice Lords from his hood in his unit that showed him, love. Malik got in the shower at the beginning of the hallway and closed the blue curtain thinking about the streets he missed.

Simone came to see him every visit, Boss would drop off tons of money for her to send him, so his commissary stayed full. He hadn't heard from Animal but Boss told him he was on a vacation because the city was on fire since the murder rate continued to rise.

Malik couldn't believe he was sitting in jail for a body he ain't even do. He never even saw Carolina when he told the police that after seeing her picture, they told him that was what all killers say.

Th sound of the shower curtains made him turn around, he saw three Vice Lords niggas rush him with big knives. He started stabbing trying to fight back but it was hopeless. The fighting and stabbing continued for 1 minute and a half, until the team ran into the shower, beating the inmates with sticks and spraying pepper spray.

Malik was on the floor bleeding everywhere by the time medical came and the nurse tried to work on him, he was not responsive and flatlined.

To Be Continued...
Chi'Raq Gangstas 2
Coming Soon

Submission Guideline

Submit the first three chapters of your completed manuscript to ldpsubmissions@gmail.com, subject line: Your book's title. The manuscript must be in a .doc file and sent as an attachment. Document should be in Times New Roman, double spaced and in size 12 font. Also, provide your synopsis and full contact information. If sending multiple submissions, they must each be in a separate email.

Have a story but no way to send it electronically? You can still submit to LDP/Ca$h Presents. Send in the first three chapters, written or typed, of your completed manuscript to:

LDP: Submissions Dept
Po Box 944
Stockbridge, Ga 30281

DO NOT send original manuscript. Must be a duplicate.

Provide your synopsis and a cover letter containing your full contact information.

Thanks for considering LDP and Ca$h Presents.

Coming Soon from Lock Down Publications/Ca$h Presents

BOW DOWN TO MY GANGSTA

By **Ca$h**

TORN BETWEEN TWO

By **Coffee**

THE STREETS STAINED MY SOUL **II**

By **Marcellus Allen**

BLOOD OF A BOSS **VI**

SHADOWS OF THE GAME II

By **Askari**

LOYAL TO THE GAME **IV**

By **T.J. & Jelissa**

IF LOVING YOU IS WRONG… **III**

By **Jelissa**

TRUE SAVAGE **VIII**

MIDNIGHT CARTEL III

DOPE BOY MAGIC IV

CITY OF KINGZ II

By **Chris Green**

BLAST FOR ME **III**

A SAVAGE DOPEBOY III

CUTTHROAT MAFIA III

DUFFLE BAG CARTEL VI

By **Ghost**

A HUSTLER'S DECEIT III

KILL ZONE **II**

BAE BELONGS TO ME III

A DOPE BOY'S QUEEN III

By **Aryanna**

Chi'Raq Gangstas

COKE KINGS V

KING OF THE TRAP II

By **T.J. Edwards**

GORILLAZ IN THE BAY V

3X KRAZY II

De'Kari

THE STREETS ARE CALLING II

Duquie Wilson

KINGPIN KILLAZ IV

STREET KINGS III

PAID IN BLOOD III

CARTEL KILLAZ IV

DOPE GODS III

Hood Rich

SINS OF A HUSTLA II

ASAD

KINGZ OF THE GAME VI

Playa Ray

SLAUGHTER GANG IV

RUTHLESS HEART IV

By Willie Slaughter

THE HEART OF A SAVAGE III

By Jibril Williams

FUK SHYT II

By Blakk Diamond

TRAP QUEEN

By Troublesome

YAYO IV

GHOST MOB

Stilloan Robinson

Romell Tukes

KINGPIN DREAMS III
By Paper Boi Rari
CREAM II
By Yolanda Moore
SON OF A DOPE FIEND III
By Renta
FOREVER GANGSTA II
GLOCKS ON SATIN SHEETS III
By Adrian Dulan
LOYALTY AIN'T PROMISED III
By Keith Williams
THE PRICE YOU PAY FOR LOVE II
By Destiny Skai
CONFESSIONS OF A GANGSTA III
By Nicholas Lock
I'M NOTHING WITHOUT HIS LOVE II
SINS OF A THUG II
By Monet Dragun
LIFE OF A SAVAGE IV
MURDA SEASON IV
GANGLAND CARTEL III
CHI'RAQ GANGSTAS II
By **Romell Tukes**
QUIET MONEY IV
THUG LIFE II
EXTENDED CLIP II
By **Trai'Quan**
THE STREETS MADE ME III
By **Larry D. Wright**
THE ULTIMATE SACRIFICE VI

194

Chi'Raq Gangstas

IF YOU CROSS ME ONCE II

ANGEL III

By **Anthony Fields**

FRIEND OR FOE III

By **Mimi**

SAVAGE STORMS II

By **Meesha**

BLOOD ON THE MONEY III

By J-Blunt

THE STREETS WILL NEVER CLOSE II

By K'ajji

NIGHTMARES OF A HUSTLA III

By King Dream

THE WIFEY I USED TO BE II

By Nicole Goosby

IN THE ARM OF HIS BOSS

By Jamila

MONEY, MURDER & MEMORIES II

Malik D. Rice

<u>**Available Now**</u>

RESTRAINING ORDER **I & II**

By **CA$H & Coffee**

LOVE KNOWS NO BOUNDARIES **I II & III**

Romell Tukes

By **Coffee**

RAISED AS A GOON I, II, III & IV

BRED BY THE SLUMS I, II, III

BLAST FOR ME I & II

ROTTEN TO THE CORE I II III

A BRONX TALE I, II, III

DUFFLE BAG CARTEL I II III IV V

HEARTLESS GOON I II III IV

A SAVAGE DOPEBOY I II

HEARTLESS GOON I II III

DRUG LORDS I II III

CUTTHROAT MAFIA I II

By **Ghost**

LAY IT DOWN **I & II**

LAST OF A DYING BREED

BLOOD STAINS OF A SHOTTA I & II III

By **Jamaica**

LOYAL TO THE GAME I II III

LIFE OF SIN I, II III

By **TJ & Jelissa**

BLOODY COMMAS I & II

SKI MASK CARTEL I II & III

KING OF NEW YORK I II,III IV V

RISE TO POWER I II III

COKE KINGS I II III IV

BORN HEARTLESS I II III IV

KING OF THE TRAP

By **T.J. Edwards**

IF LOVING HIM IS WRONG…I & II

LOVE ME EVEN WHEN IT HURTS I II III

Chi'Raq Gangstas

By **Jelissa**
WHEN THE STREETS CLAP BACK I & II III
THE HEART OF A SAVAGE I II
By **Jibril Williams**
A DISTINGUISHED THUG STOLE MY HEART I II & III
LOVE SHOULDN'T HURT I II III IV
RENEGADE BOYS I II III IV
PAID IN KARMA I II III
SAVAGE STORMS
By **Meesha**
A GANGSTER'S CODE I &, II III
A GANGSTER'S SYN I II III
THE SAVAGE LIFE I II III
CHAINED TO THE STREETS I II III
BLOOD ON THE MONEY I II
By J-Blunt
PUSH IT TO THE LIMIT
By **Bre' Hayes**
BLOOD OF A BOSS **I, II, III, IV, V**
SHADOWS OF THE GAME
By **Askari**
THE STREETS BLEED MURDER **I, II & III**
THE HEART OF A GANGSTA I II& III
By **Jerry Jackson**
CUM FOR ME I II III IV V VI
An **LDP Erotica Collaboration**
BRIDE OF A HUSTLA **I II & II**
THE FETTI GIRLS **I, II& III**
CORRUPTED BY A GANGSTA I, II III, IV
BLINDED BY HIS LOVE

THE PRICE YOU PAY FOR LOVE

DOPE GIRL MAGIC I II III

By **Destiny Skai**

WHEN A GOOD GIRL GOES BAD

By **Adrienne**

THE COST OF LOYALTY I II III

By Kweli

A GANGSTER'S REVENGE **I II III & IV**

THE BOSS MAN'S DAUGHTERS I II III IV V

A SAVAGE LOVE **I & II**

BAE BELONGS TO ME I II

A HUSTLER'S DECEIT I, II, III

WHAT BAD BITCHES DO I, II, III

SOUL OF A MONSTER I II III

KILL ZONE

A DOPE BOY'S QUEEN I II

By **Aryanna**

A KINGPIN'S AMBITON

A KINGPIN'S AMBITION **II**

I MURDER FOR THE DOUGH

By **Ambitious**

TRUE SAVAGE I II III IV V VI VII

DOPE BOY MAGIC I, II, III

MIDNIGHT CARTEL I II

CITY OF KINGZ

By **Chris Green**

A DOPEBOY'S PRAYER

By **Eddie "Wolf" Lee**

THE KING CARTEL **I, II & III**

By **Frank Gresham**

Chi'Raq Gangstas

THESE NIGGAS AIN'T LOYAL **I, II & III**

By **Nikki Tee**

GANGSTA SHYT **I II &III**

By **CATO**

THE ULTIMATE BETRAYAL

By **Phoenix**

BOSS'N UP **I , II & III**

By **Royal Nicole**

I LOVE YOU TO DEATH

By Destiny J

I RIDE FOR MY HITTA

I STILL RIDE FOR MY HITTA

By **Misty Holt**

LOVE & CHASIN' PAPER

By **Qay Crockett**

TO DIE IN VAIN

SINS OF A HUSTLA

By **ASAD**

BROOKLYN HUSTLAZ

By **Boogsy Morina**

BROOKLYN ON LOCK I & II

By **Sonovia**

GANGSTA CITY

By **Teddy Duke**

A DRUG KING AND HIS DIAMOND I & II III

A DOPEMAN'S RICHES

HER MAN, MINE'S TOO I, II

CASH MONEY HO'S

THE WIFEY I USED TO BE

By Nicole Goosby

TRAPHOUSE KING **I II & III**

KINGPIN KILLAZ I II III

STREET KINGS I II

PAID IN BLOOD **I II**

CARTEL KILLAZ I II III

DOPE GODS I II

By **Hood Rich**

LIPSTICK KILLAH **I, II, III**

CRIME OF PASSION I II & III

FRIEND OR FOE I II

By **Mimi**

STEADY MOBBN' **I, II, III**

THE STREETS STAINED MY SOUL

By **Marcellus Allen**

WHO SHOT YA **I, II, III**

SON OF A DOPE FIEND I II

Renta

GORILLAZ IN THE BAY **I II III IV**

TEARS OF A GANGSTA I II

3X KRAZY

DE'KARI

TRIGGADALE I II III

Elijah R. Freeman

GOD BLESS THE TRAPPERS I, II, III

THESE SCANDALOUS STREETS I, II, III

FEAR MY GANGSTA I, II, III IV, V

THESE STREETS DON'T LOVE NOBODY I, II

BURY ME A G I, II, III, IV, V

A GANGSTA'S EMPIRE I, II, III, IV

THE DOPEMAN'S BODYGAURD I II

Chi'Raq Gangstas

THE REALEST KILLAZ I II III
Tranay Adams
THE STREETS ARE CALLING
Duquie Wilson
MARRIED TO A BOSS... I II III
By Destiny Skai & Chris Green
KINGZ OF THE GAME I II III IV V
Playa Ray
SLAUGHTER GANG I II III
RUTHLESS HEART I II III
By Willie Slaughter
FUK SHYT
By Blakk Diamond
DON'T F#CK WITH MY HEART I II
By Linnea
ADDICTED TO THE DRAMA I II III
IN THE ARM OF HIS BOSS II
By Jamila
YAYO I II III
A SHOOTER'S AMBITION I II
By S. Allen
TRAP GOD I II III
By Troublesome
FOREVER GANGSTA
GLOCKS ON SATIN SHEETS I II
By Adrian Dulan
TOE TAGZ I II III
By Ah'Million
KINGPIN DREAMS I II
By Paper Boi Rari

CONFESSIONS OF A GANGSTA I II

By Nicholas Lock

I'M NOTHING WITHOUT HIS LOVE

SINS OF A THUG

By Monet Dragun

CAUGHT UP IN THE LIFE I II III

By Robert Baptiste

NEW TO MONEY, MURDER & MEMORIES

THE GAME I II III

By **Malik D. Rice**

LIFE OF A SAVAGE I II III

A GANGSTA'S QUR'AN I II III

MURDA SEASON I II III

GANGLAND CARTEL I II

CHI'RAQ GANGSTAS

By **Romell Tukes**

LOYALTY AIN'T PROMISED I II

By Keith Williams

QUIET MONEY I II III

THUG LIFE

EXTENDED CLIP

By **Trai'Quan**

THE STREETS MADE ME I II

By **Larry D. Wright**

THE ULTIMATE SACRIFICE I, II, III, IV, V

KHADIFI

IF YOU CROSS ME ONCE

ANGEL I II

By **Anthony Fields**

THE LIFE OF A HOOD STAR

Chi'Raq Gangstas

By Ca$h & Rashia Wilson

THE STREETS WILL NEVER CLOSE

By K'ajji

CREAM

By Yolanda Moore

NIGHTMARES OF A HUSTLA I II

By King Dream

Romell Tukes

BOOKS BY LDP'S CEO, CA$H

TRUST IN NO MAN

TRUST IN NO MAN 2

TRUST IN NO MAN 3

BONDED BY BLOOD

SHORTY GOT A THUG

THUGS CRY

THUGS CRY 2

THUGS CRY 3

TRUST NO BITCH

TRUST NO BITCH 2

TRUST NO BITCH 3

TIL MY CASKET DROPS

RESTRAINING ORDER

RESTRAINING ORDER 2

IN LOVE WITH A CONVICT

LIFE OF A HOOD STAR

Chi'Raq Gangstas

CPSIA information can be obtained
at www.ICGtesting.com
Printed in the USA
LVHW051254140221
679287LV00010B/1265